# THE WAITING TIME...

## Margaret Carr

# CHIVERS

**British Library Cataloguing in Publication Data available**

This Large Print edition published by BBC Audiobooks Ltd, Bath, 2009.
Published by arrangement with the Author.

U.K. Hardcover ISBN 978 1 408 41275 6
U.K. Softcover ISBN 978 1 408 41276 3

Printed and bound in Great Britain by
CPI Antony Rowe, Chippenham, Wiltshire

# CHAPTER ONE

Jenny Carson shook the rain from her hair and looked up at the timetable on the notice-board. Because she was late, the entrance hall of the Humanities Building was nearly empty. Pinned to the pigeon-hole beneath the board was a large note—J. CARSON, CALL AT OFFICE.

She tapped on the office door and went in. 'Yes?'

The older of the secretaries scowled at her over the top of her half-lens reading glasses.

'Jenny Carson, there's a notice on the board for me to call in.'

'Carson, did you say, third year?'

Jenny nodded. The woman pushed back her chair with a disgruntled sigh and, getting up, moved to the back of the room. Jenny scanned the secretarial lecture rota. The name of one lecturer had been scratched through. Did that mean the lecture was cancelled, or was someone else taking it, Jenny wondered. She was annoyed because her lodgings were six miles away, a bus fare she could barely afford and she'd endured a soaking she would rather have been without. Ella Vane was her favourite tutor and an excellent lecturer which was why she had made the effort to come in today.

'Yes, I thought I'd seen something, here it is,' the secretary said on her return to the desk.

The smile stiffened on Jenny's face as she stretched out a hand for the brown envelope with the distinctive black scrawl emblazoned across it. She pushed the envelope down into the bottom of her damp pocket. It always came to the flat by post. Why suddenly should he take to sending it here? It had been delivered by hand which was even more puzzling.

She eased the dampness from her shoulders as she tried to catch the secretary's attention.

'Can you tell me who is taking the secretarial lecture?'

'It's in Lecture Theatre Two and you've missed half of it already. The lecturer is a Mr Ryder Surtees.'

Jenny stepped backward as the shock hit her like a physical blow.

'Are you all right?' the secretary enquired, a wary look in her eyes. 'You girls don't look after yourselves. Have you had anything to eat today?'

'Yes, thank you,' Jenny whispered. 'I think I'll give the lecture a miss, thank you.'

Still in a daze she stumbled from the building. Outside the rain had ceased and a sharp wind was keeping it at bay. Jenny shivered. Was there any way she could have misunderstood what the secretary had said? There couldn't be two men of that name. She took the envelope from the depths of her

2

pocket and straightened it out. The script of old Reginald Surtees, still so strong and defined, like his son's, stared back at her, no stamp, no address, just her name.

Three more people jostled in behind her in the bus shelter and she moved up to the front. The first green town bus hissed straight past but the second drew up alongside the shelter and disgorged several people on to the pavement as Jenny stepped aboard. She tripped over someone's feet on her way down the aisle and as she sank into her seat the cold from the damp anorak seeped into her back.

At exactly twelve thirty, little Helen Carson burst in through the front door of the flat.

'Mummy, Mummy, guess what? Anna Mitchell is having a party tomorrow and I can go.'

'Can you now!'

Jenny laughed as she stooped to catch the little girl and swing her up into her arms. The plump woman turning to close the front door caught the look in Jenny's eyes, above the little girl's small head, and smiled.

'And Patty says she'll stay with me, won't you, Patty?' the child added.

Then without waiting for a reply from the older woman the small head tipped to one side and pansy eyes stared into Jenny's.

'If you can't come, that is.'

'Well, it just so happens, young lady, that I can come, so what do you think of that?'

'Oh, cool,' she cried, dancing off as soon as Jenny set her back on her feet.

'You're back earlier than expected,' Patty said.

'Yes, the lecture was cancelled and I got a thorough soaking.'

'Umm, you look a bit flushed. Perhaps I should keep tomorrow afternoon free after all just in case you don't make it to the party of the year.'

They both started to laugh as Helen danced back into the living-room demanding, 'What will I wear Mummy, for Anna's party?'

After tea there was a great sorting through of Helen's clothes in an effort to find the proper dress for the forthcoming party. A decision was reached at last and then nothing would do but a bath in Mummy's best bubble bath.

The following morning was Saturday and Jenny woke with a niggling headache and the beginnings of a sore throat. She grumbled to herself as she raised her aching limbs from the bed and along the passage to the bathroom.

'Mummy, I can't find my clean socks.'

Jenny groaned.

'Just put your jump-suit and slippers on for now. You don't have to get dressed up until after lunch.'

Jenny bent down to put the plug in the bath, then straightened up with a hand clutching her forehead. The face in the mirror above the handbasin looked decidedly unpromising. She shook two tablets from a bottle of aspirin and swallowed them with the aid of a glass of water, determined not to let the onset of a cold spoil the day for Helen.

'Anna's mummy and daddy are very rich and live in a big house with servants. When they lived abroad, Anna had her party in the garden but it's too cold here. Her daddy has just come back from 'merica and he brought her a cool doll, nearly as tall as she is. Her name is Irma.'

The little voice went on and on as Jenny tied her plaits with toggles.

'I told her my daddy worked abroad as well and that he hadn't been home for ages, but we have a photograph of him, don't we Mummy, so I'll know him when he comes home.'

They even made it on the bus with the little voice prattling on! Jenny's heart sank for she had never plucked up the courage to tell her daughter the truth about the picture she had found one day in one of Jenny's drawers. The bus put them down in Chester Gardens and they walked slowly along the road of large, detached houses looking for the name of Anna's house.

The drive of the house called Greenacres was blocked solid with cars as was the kerb alongside the entrance. Jenny and Helen threaded their way past the cars and arrived on the doorstep just as the door was opened by a thin girl in a white apron. The girl put out a complaining cat and shooed it off before inviting mother and daughter inside. Relieved of their coats they were met by a plump five-year-old who immediately took Helen off to meet Irma, the doll.

Jenny hesitated in the hall then followed them into the room where the noise of other children could be heard. A girl in a grey and white overall came up to Jenny, smiling.

'Hello, there. The nannies are next door. Helen will be quite all right with us. You go off and have a cup of tea and a chat.'

Jenny backed out, too shy to admit to being a mother and not a nanny. A room full of gossiping nannies did not appeal and she wondered if she could safely leave and come back later. She looked around for the girl in the apron but she had disappeared. Well, she couldn't leave without finding out what time the party was due to break up. Jenny walked towards the next door down the hall and opened it.

The chatter stilled and a cheery voice called, 'There's a seat over here.'

'Thank you, but I'm not staying. Could you please tell me what time the party is expected to break up?'

Her question startled the room full of women, then the cheery girl spoke again.

'Oh, well, about four I should think.'

She glanced around the room for confirmation and there was a low rustle of murmured agreement.

As Jenny walked away from the house the worries about the reappearance of Ryder Surtees in her life surged once more to the fore. There had been nothing but the usual monthly cheque in the envelope from Mr Surtees senior, everything exactly as it always was except that it had been delivered by hand to the college.

Sitting in a café with a cooling cup of coffee before her Jenny noticed a local newspaper lying on the vacant chair next to her. Perhaps there was something in the paper about the lectures, Jenny thought, for after all he was a name to be reckoned with now. Sure enough, on the fifth page there was a large advertisement about a series of lectures to be given at the college by the well known Literary Critic, Ryder Surtees. The series was to consist of twice-weekly lectures over the following four weeks. Jenny let go a sigh of relief. Only four weeks, if she could avoid him for the next month this terrible threat from her past would be over.

There were eight weeks to go before the beginning of her finals at which time her allowance from Reginald Surtees would end. Until then, however, she would have to tread very carefully. She could allow nothing to endanger her plans. She glanced at her watch. It was still only three o'clock and it would take no more than ten minutes to walk back to the house in Chester Gardens. She picked up the paper and began to read. The local news was not startling until she reached the back page and glanced at the obituaries.

When her head cleared and she read again the name at the top of the first column her whole body was shaking so hard she couldn't trust herself to fold the paper and put it out of sight. Reginald Surtees was dead! This was what had brought Ryder home.

Her headache throbbed with every foot she put to the pavement as she made her way back to collect Helen. Limbs that had dully ached this morning now cracked stiffly and her throat felt red raw and dry as sawdust. With her mind so clouded with problems she nearly walked passed the house. Nannies with their charges were spilling out of the front door and into the waiting cars. A tall, expensively-dressed woman some ten years Jenny's senior stepped forward as she entered the hall.

'Ah, Mrs Carson, I am so sorry you were mistaken for a nanny. I do hope you will forgive us. We had no idea you were bringing Helen yourself. Please accept our apologies.'

Jenny took the proffered hand and smiled.

'Is Helen ready?' she asked, searching the hall for her daughter's face.

'Of course, she's in the conservatory with Anna. Your daughter was very taken with a friend of ours who stopped by for tea.'

Jenny was following Anna's mother through

the house when Mrs Mitchell asked, 'Have you heard of Ryder Surtees?'

Jenny froze.

'He and my husband were colleagues in America.'

She turned round when she realised Jenny was no longer behind her. 'Is something wrong, Mrs Carson?'

'No, I'm in rather a hurry though so if you could just tell Helen.'

The woman gave her a curious glance then, turning back to the door at the far end of the hall, called the girls. Helen was flushed but silent as she came into the hall and took hold of Jenny's hand.

'Say thank you, Helen,' Jenny reminded her.

'Thank you very much for the party.'

'My pleasure,' Mrs Mitchell murmured, then turning to her daughter said, 'Show your friend out, dear.'

The journey home was quiet. When they entered the flat and Jenny had switched on the fire and hung up their coats, Helen was still quiet. Jenny began to worry that there was more than just tiredness involved.

'Is something wrong, Helen?' she asked, sitting down in an armchair and pulling the little girl on to her lap. 'Didn't you enjoy the party?'

'Ye-es.'

'Was someone nasty to you?'

'No-o.'

'Then what is it, darling?' Jenny persisted.

'Mummy.'

'Yes.'

'When is Daddy coming home?'

Jenny bit down hard on a trembling lip and tried to smile. The time had come when she was least ready for it.

'Helen, Daddy isn't coming home. When he went to America, he and Mummy decided that his work was too important for him to stay with us any more so he lives on his own now.'

There was a frown between her daughter's fine brows.

'Where does he live then?'

Jenny was surprised by the question.

'Well, in a hotel I suppose.'

'Which hotel?'

'I don't know, why?'

Helen wriggled off her knee and stood facing her with a look that saw right through her and dared her to tell anything but the truth. The firm lines of the mouth that the baby bow shape could not disguise and the straight stare that were all Ryder's were turned on her in full force.

'I saw my daddy today.'

Helen ran off and came back with the snapshot from her bedside table.

'Is this my daddy?'

Jenny drew a tight breath.

'Yes.'

Helen beamed.

'I knew he was my daddy. Anna said he wasn't 'cause he didn't have a wife and he looks a little bit different.'

Jenny took hold of her daughter's thin shoulders.

'Helen, did you speak to the man?'

'No, he was going away. Anna's mummy said not to bother him.'

She started to sob and Jenny at a loss for words pulled her close.

Later that night Jenny sat in front of the electric fire, a glass of whisky and hot lemonade in her hands, trying to work out how she could complete the last eight weeks of study without the help of Reginald Surtees' cheques. She had been putting money by to cover a possible time lapse between leaving college and taking up full-time employment and she didn't want to have to dip into this fund. Perhaps a part-time job if she could fine one. Patty lived in the ground floor flat and would always babysit which was a great help.

There was the possibility, of course, that the remaining two cheques would be covered by the estate. That depended upon who it was handling his affairs. The real problem, she reflected wearily, was how soon the knowledge of these payments would filter back to Ryder and what would happen when they did. How would he react when he discovered his father had been paying for the education of the wife he had ditched when a lucrative job had been dangled under his nose. He would have to be stupid not to put two and two together, Jenny thought, worrying at her bottom lip, and stupid was one thing Ryder Surtees was not.

On Monday morning, Jenny took Helen to nursery school before calling around at a fellow student's flat. Tim had been a great help to her in the past and was a loyal friend.

'I wonder if you have the programme for the Surtees' lectures,' she asked him as she pushed passed him in the hall.

He was still in his dressing-gown with a bacon sandwich in one hand while the other hand tried to flatten his spiky hair.

'Sure, I have it around somewhere. Why don't you look for it while I get dressed?'

Jenny nodded and started searching through piles of books and leaflets scattered across the table and several chairs.

'The first one was great,' he called through the open doorway, 'but I don't remember seeing you there on Friday.'

'No, I didn't go. I'm trying to steer clear of the college until I get rid of this cold.'

She found what she wanted as Tim came back into the room. 'Staying for a coffee?' he asked.

'Umm, thanks, I might as well.'

'How's things?'

'I'm looking for a part-time job actually, so tell me if you hear of anything.'

Tim smiled, shaking his head at the same

12

time.

'You're a funny thing. Why wait until the run-up to the finals to want a job?'

'My uncle died, so the allowance will probably stop.'

Tim had always been led to believe in the tale of the rich uncle and his face twisted with sympathy now.

'Well, I'll keep my eyes and ears open and if I hear anything I'll let you know.'

'Thanks, Tim.'

'Will Patty babysit for you?'

'I haven't asked her yet, but it should be all right.'

'Well, if I can be of any use, just whistle.'

It was nearly two weeks before a clerking job in a small building firm became vacant and Jenny was settling in nicely when Helen broke her arm at nursery school.

Jenny was working round the clock now with study, housework, part-time job and a fractious little girl to look after. She could feel the stress building up inside her and was powerless to do anything about it. The cold that had never really cleared lay on her chest for too long. She became so tired that even when Helen went back to school she couldn't ease up for fear of losing her grip on reality altogether and retiring to bed never to rise again.

She went into college as little as possible and in the time since Helen had mentioned him, she had neither seen nor heard from Ryder Surtees.

## CHAPTER TWO

Jenny's project was scattered all over the floor one evening when the doorbell rang, and she found Tim on the doorstep. 'May I come in?' he asked.

'Sure,' Jenny said, stepping backward. 'I'm not quite with it, I'm afraid. I'm in the middle of some work.'

Tim strode passed her into the living-room.

'Watch your feet,' she warned, as Tim found himself a spare armchair and sat down.

'Won't you take your coat off?' she asked.

'I'm not staying, Jenny. I only stopped by to let you know what great lectures you were missing.'

'The Surtees' lectures?'

'What else? What are you playing at, Jenny? You come round to my place to get the programme then don't even bother to turn up.'

'I have my reasons, Tim.'

'Aren't you going to any of them?'

'No, it's difficult getting the time and Patty isn't always available. Besides, I don't have to give you my reasons.'

'Why not? I'm always there for you, aren't I? These lectures could make a heck of a

14

difference in the finals.'

'Oh, I doubt that, Tim.'

She gave a rough laugh that ended in a cough.

'I have more faith in myself than to lay my life's hopes at the feet of Ryder Surtees.'

Tim frowned, his eyes never leaving Jenny's face.

'That's not like you,' he said, sounding puzzled.

Jenny struggled to pull herself together. She was very fond of Tim. She owed him more than a bout of bad temper. It had been Tim who had introduced her to Patty when Jenny had been desperate for accommodation. Patty far from ostracising her for having a baby in tow, saw it as a heaven-sent opportunity to indulge her own childless maternal urges. In the past four and half years, Patty had taken the place of Helen's grandmother and although Jack, Patty's husband, paid less attention to the little girl, she looked on him automatically as a grandfather. Tim was the beloved uncle she could twist around her little finger.

'I'm sorry, Tim, I'm just tired, I suppose.'

'I'll take turn about with Helen for the lectures if that will help.'

'No, Tim, but thanks anyway.'

'But . . .'

'That's my last word, Tim.'

He shrugged his shoulders and climbed to

his feet.

'Well, I best be going.'

Jenny saw him to the door.

'Don't forget, Jenny, if you want to talk, I'm the best listener around.'

His grin was full of gentle self-effacement. On impulse Jenny leaned forward and kissed his cheek.

'I know,' she said, then he was gone.

Was she really missing out by not attending the lectures, she wondered. Ryder had been a local journalist when she first met him at a student demonstration for a ban on the shipment of live animals. He'd singled her out for a personal interview and been a sympathetic and interested listener to her enthusiastic offerings on the subject.

He'd sat on the corner of a table in the Student's Union Hall, swinging a long cord-clad leg and every now and again a hand would flick back a lock of brown hair that persisted in falling forward over his brow. His smile lightened the dark brown of his eyes and caught the corners of a straight mouth above a strong chin. It had been a short step from that interview to the dates that followed.

When he'd asked her out that first time to see a film they were both interested and her thoughts had been of sheer disbelief that a handsome, knowledgeable professional would find something interesting in herself. As their knowledge of each other increased, common

16

ground was found; their love of literature, music and the countryside, something that could be shared, plus a sense of humour that often excluded the people around them.

She hadn't been alone in her attraction to him, for all females found him fascinating. The fact that even then he was a man in his thirties and she a student of nineteen never bothered them, although it frequently gave rise to comments from others. He delighted in her thirst for knowledge and gave her every encouragement in her ambition to study linguistics.

They married six months after that first interview and she moved into his home. At that point in time, Ryder still lived with his father in the house he'd lived in all his life.

Jenny, shy and unsure of herself, had accepted the large draughty house with its dark wallpaper and varnished skirting. Anything was better than the tiny flat she shared with two other girls neither of whom were people she would have chosen as friends in other circumstances.

Reginald Surtees, Ryder's father, was a retired businessman who had been a widower for twenty years. He kept very much to himself, only joining them for the occasional meal. His manner was pleasant if negative to his young daughter-in-law while he expressed a stubborn reluctance to her interference in any change to the running of the home.

Their dour housekeeper of indeterminate age and tiny stature refused point blank any effort on Jenny's part to help with housework or cooking, even grumbling when Jenny made herself toast before leaving for college.

Whenever Ryder was away chasing a story for the paper, Jenny would stay out late with friends rather than go back alone to the cold house and people in it. Loving Ryder had felt so right. In his arms she had learned the power of give and take, woken to a loving that hurt in its need for reciprocation.

Once married, however, he seemed to have less time for her than prior to their quiet registry office wedding. His job was taking him away more all the time. They had frequent discussions about moving away once Jenny qualified. But that seemed so far off and Jenny was left with only the company of ghostly Reginald and the dour housekeeper.

When Ryder came home one evening and spun her around in his arms, with a huge smile across his face and broke the news that he had been offered a wonderful opportunity in America with a television company, Jenny had been equally excited for him. But as the following days passed and she became more aware of what the American job entailed, her eagerness cooled. She tried to voice her worries but all her efforts were brushed aside for this wonderful future that had presented itself. That he failed to sense Jenny's frustration and unhappiness added to her worries. She wanted a home of her own and in America there would only be a series of rented rooms waiting for them with the possibility of several moves.

Her career also was important to her and if they were to be travelling how was she to continue with her course work? She loved Ryder to distraction. But when, after several weeks of worry and unanswered questions, she was told bluntly that he was going and that she must decide one way or the other, she had dug her heels in and asked for more time. Then Ryder had coldly, and without concern, called it a day.

If, in the months following Ryder's departure, it hadn't been for the awareness of Helen growing inside her, Jenny would have faded from the world without a ripple. When Reginald was informed of the coming baby he immediately took control of the situation and sent her off to a private nursing home. Life and death decisions were taken from her and slowly she began to regain her health and strength.

Jenny now took a deep, quivering breath. That was all a long time ago and she was no longer an impressionable teenager. She would be twenty-five next month and had nothing to worry about from the likes of Ryder Surtees. Surely it was silly to deprive herself of these lectures on some fanciful idea that Ryder might try to take Helen from her, when in truth his reaction would possibly be the very opposite.

When Jenny told Tim of her change of heart and promised to accompany him to the next Surtees lecture his relieved grin made her laugh.

'Gimme one,' he said, slapping his open palm on hers and sending shock waves all the way up her arm.

So, on the following Tuesday, after making sure Patty could have Helen, Jenny accompanied Tim to the college. A cheeky sun was poking between high clouds as she and Tim stepped down from the bus. In the park across the road from the college's main entrance daffodils covered the grass with colour. It had been a cold, wet spring but now the mornings and evenings were stretching out and soon the sun would be generating more heat. She felt a surge of well-being flow through her. Tim took her bag from her grasp and took hold of her hand.

'We'll have to hurry if we want to get decent seats.'

They hurried through the main hall, up the stairs and right to the new extension. It was only two years old and housed two new lecture theatres, with low ceilings. It swept around in a wide semi-circle, with comfortable, individual seating and an amplification system that owed everything to modern technology.

Jenny allowed Tim to find their seats, then sat down pulling the little writing rest over her knees. She was acknowledging other friends when two men strode down the aisle and mounted the platform. Ted Harrison, head of Humanities, walked up to the table at the front of the platform and began his introduction, while the second figure seated himself in a director's chair at the back.

'This is the fourth of eight lectures. Now, ladies and gentlemen, Mr Ryder Surtees.'

There was much clapping as Ryder stood up and came forward from the shadows. Thanking Mr Harrison, he came out in front of the table and leaned back until he was sitting on the edge, one foot a few inches from the ground. His head remained bent for a few moments to allow his audience to satisfy their curiosity then he looked up into the sea of waiting faces.

Jenny, after her first quick look, kept her eyes firmly on her notepad. By the end of the lecture her body ached from head to foot with the tension in her muscles. Now was the time to be noticed, when at the end of a lecture a short period was thrown open for questions. The speaker would search the faces above him and concentrate on the area from which the question came. Defying her stiff neck Jenny bent it even farther and scribbled like mad. She was horrified therefore when she saw from the corner of her eye Tim's hand go up.

'The gentleman over there.'

She heard the familiar voice directing everyone's attention towards them. Quickly she bent over her table rest and foraged in the bag at her feet.

'Perhaps if the person next to you stopped delving in her bag I could hear your question,' Ryder was saying.

The shock to Jenny was like a douche of cold water and had the effect of making her sit bolt upright. Mortified, she listened to Tim repeat his question. Ryder answered it, his tone calm and authoritative, his eyes cool and intelligent with no sign of recognition. Now it was over and they were filing out, Jenny let go a sigh of relief.

'Yes, it was good, wasn't it?' Tim said misinterpreting her sigh. 'You must have taken more notes in that one lecture than I have over the lot.'

'There was more to it than I thought.'

Jenny allowed Tim to persuade her to go for coffee. On the bus back to the flat there was quite a crowd. When she finally reached home, Patty and Helen had tea ready and it wasn't until Helen was in bed and Patty returned to her own flat that Jenny had time to reflect about her first sight of Ryder Surtees in five years. Tall, well over six feet, slim, though his slimness had always been that of an athlete rather than plain thinness. Today though, his slimness had revealed a gaunt quality that had been missing five years ago and a neat haircut unable to hide the grey threads. The deep brown eyes were Helen's eyes though they lacked his daughter's soft warmth. She let the picture of him drift through her mind, renewing a loneliness she'd thought long since buried.

The relief the end of Ryder's lectures brought to Jenny was quickly squashed when on her way out through the hall she once again caught sight of a note asking her to call at the office. The envelope with the thick black scrawl was laid on the desk and Jenny picked it up and thrust it into her pocket, but not before Tim had seen it.

'Look, I hope you don't mind my asking but wasn't that Surtees' writing on that envelope?'

They were on their way up to her flat and she was able to reply without guilt.

'No, it isn't, it's my uncle's.'

'But I thought your uncle was dead.'

'So he is, but he must have left the last two allowances ready for delivery. The regular cheque is not due for another week yet.'

Tim shrugged, then the door at the top of the stairs opened and Helen gave a squeal of pleasure at the sight of her favourite person and all queries about the cheque were forgotten. Tea that day was a fun meal. Patty disappeared after tea and reappeared just in time for Helen's bath, while Jenny and Tim went off to the cinema.

It was the next morning before Jenny
had a chance to open the envelope containing
the cheque, the amount covering the
remaining two months' allowances. She rushed
downstairs to tell Patty. This meant that with
her part-time job, the gap between her finals
and taking full-time employment was secure.
She could have kissed the fates, she was so
giddy with relief.

Patty was happy for her, clucking away
behind the sheet she was folding after her
ironing.

'About time your luck changed,' she said,
watching the blonde head bobbing about
behind the sheet. 'Now all you want is some
good news from that job you wrote away
about.'

'Oh, just imagine, Patty, if I was to get an
interview for that local teaching post
everything would just fall into place. I could
keep an eye on Helen during school hours and
we could stay here with you for the time
being.'

Patty watched the slight figure of the girl
who had brought so much love into her
life, her fair hair waving naturally over her
shoulders and grey eyes full of cloudy promise.
A straight nose divided an oval face and her
mouth lifted sweetly when she smiled, as she
was now.

'Jenny, when the good lord looks down and
sees how things stand, why he'll have so much

to make up to you, you'll be happy for the rest of your life.'

Her eyes glittered with tears.

'I'm not looking forward to the day you move on but I'll be happy to see you really settled with a good husband, a career and more family to keep the little one company.'

Jenny wrapped her arms around the older woman and buried her face in the ample bosom.

'I'm not away yet, Patty. First I must get a good pass.'

'You will, dear. I feel it in my bones and you know how right they always are.'

'Thank you, Patty, for all your support. I couldn't have got this far if it wasn't for you. Now I must get to work or I'll lose the part-time job I already have and all the glee will have been for nothing.'

She was on her way out when Patty called.

'By the way, Jenny, there was a woman here yesterday looking for you. A Mrs Mitchell she said her name was.'

Jenny's hand stilled on the door knob.

'Mrs Mitchell? Did she say what she wanted?'

'No, just that she was the mother of one of Helen's friends.'

'Thank you, Patty.'

The bubble of excitement had burst.

Meanwhile, Helen's fracture was healing nicely, sister informed her, during a visit to the

25

local hospital. Helen had been indignant because she had not been given a pot plaster for her friends to draw on but only a stiff splint to support her arm during its healing process. The splint she could take off at inconvenient times like bathtime and bedtime. It had a Velcro fastening and was easy for her to adjust herself.

A few days later Helen came home after nursery school without it. Jenny was very cross to think that the teacher had allowed her to take it off. On this particular day Anna's nanny had collected both children from school at lunchtime, as they only attended half days and had brought Helen home at teatime after she had been playing with Anna during the afternoon.

'I didn't leave it at school, Mummy,' Helen said, with a look of great concentration. 'I left it at Anna's. She wanted to try it on.'

Jenny looked down at her daughter's defiant expression and said, 'Well, I suppose we can always get it back tomorrow as we know where it is.'

She wasn't happy at the thought of a trip to the Mitchells', but she was curious as to why Mrs Mitchell had called at the flat.

'Maybe nanny will find it and bring it to school tomorrow,' Helen offered.

Jenny's flat was housed in an old building and although the rooms had been large and spacious once, they were now divided many

26

times over by plasterboard. With the exception of the living-room, the other four rooms were extremely poky. So Jenny's cry of exasperation when she stood in the entrance of Helen's tiny bedroom that evening and saw the entire contents of her daughter's drawers covered the floor was not unexpected to Helen.

'I can't find it, Mummy, I can't find my daddy's picture,' the child wailed.

Together they tidied the room searching for the photograph as they went.

'When did you last have it?' Jenny asked her daughter.

'I showed it to Anna's mummy when she came to talk to Patty. That was when she asked me to tea, but I'm sure she gave it back.'

Jenny's mouth was a sharp line against her pale face, but what could she say to a five-year-old? She had never regretted anything so much in all her life as allowing Helen to find and keep that photograph. Ryder knew nothing of Helen's birth for Jenny had been in the very earliest stages of pregnancy when he left and she had sworn Reginald to secrecy, for the good of his son's career, she had told him and he had agreed. No wonder Mrs Mitchell had not returned to see her. If she had been curious about Helen's reaction to the sight of Ryder, she had her answer now.

That night Jenny walked the floor until the early hours of the morning. Would the woman keep it to herself, or would she have shown the picture to Ryder by now? For Jenny had no doubt that was where the missing photograph was. What a mess she fretted. She would just have to brazen it out tomorrow, go around to the house, ask for Helen's arm support and the photograph all in the same breath, then beat a hasty retreat and hope that Ryder never got to hear of it. With a bit of luck he would be out of the country again by now.

Anna's nanny met Jenny at the school gate next morning and returned the splint, thus spiking Jenny's plans. She decided to phone Mrs Mitchell only to be told, when she did so, that Mrs Mitchell was in London. Eventually, forcing herself to put matters aside for the time being, she settled down to study. Time slipped passed unnoticed. When she eased back once more and stretched her arms she could hear Helen's voice, shrill with excitement, on the staircase outside.

Patty's getting an earful today, she thought with a smile, as she put her books to one side and went to welcome her daughter.

The door swung open and Helen cried, 'Look, Mummy! I've brought Daddy home.'

# CHAPTER THREE

The shock took Jenny's breath away and had her step back against the table next to her chair. 'Hello, Jennifer, it's been a long time. I take it this visit is entirely unexpected,' he said softly.

Jenny glanced at Helen, whose face shone with excitement.

'My daddy came with Anna's daddy to pick her up. He doesn't remember me but that's because I was little when he left, isn't it, Mummy?'

Jenny had never deliberately lied to Helen. She'd omitted information, yes, but this time she was cornered.

'Yes, dear. Now go downstairs and let Patty know what's happened,' she said, praying Patty would know what was being asked of her.

Helen hesitated, looking all the way up the length of her father's figure. 'You won't go away, will you?'

Jenny held her breath.

'I'll be here when you get back,' Ryder said, giving the little girl a gentle smile.

The smile disappeared once the door shut behind her. He turned back to Jenny with a frown.

'Why, Jennifer? Wouldn't the father support her? Was that why you blackmailed my father into paying for your education?'

Jenny couldn't believe her ears. He didn't recognise his own daughter! How could he reject her when she looked so like him?

'I realised what was happening when I went through his papers. He obviously believed you so I didn't see any point in stopping the last two payments. I knew you were the kind of person to fight a setback, so I wish you well in your finals.'

'Thank you,' she said.

Perhaps it was just as well he didn't believe what Helen had obviously told him, but how she was going to explain his disinterest to a five-year-old she dreaded to think.

He was looking around the flat, distaste plain in his eyes. It was all she could do not to tell him to go, but remembering his promise to Helen, she offered him a seat and a cup of tea. He declined the tea and Jenny sat on the edge of an old rocking-chair she'd picked up in a second-hand shop a couple of years earlier.

The silence was wired with static until Ryder crossed his long legs and asked, 'Why my photograph? Didn't you have one of her father's?'

You are her father, she screamed silently, then shook her head.

'Well, you are going to have to tell her the truth now. I fly back to America at the weekend.'

'Where are you staying?'

'Why?'

Jenny shrugged.

'Just in case she asks.'

He smiled then.

'I get the impression that if she found out she might very well come and claim me again.'

Doesn't that tell you something, Jenny cried to herself. Can't you hear yourself in your daughter? Jenny gave a sad shake of her head then stiffened her spine and gave him a direct look.

'She won't.'

Heavy lids fell covering his eyes as he said, 'You can contact me at the International.'

To Jenny's immense relief Patty's heavy footsteps could be heard on the landing as Helen scrabbled to open the door.

'This is my daddy,' she said to Patty, before running across the room and flinging herself at her mother.

Patty was signalling to Jenny over the back of Ryder's head that she was sorry to interrupt but could delay Helen no longer. Ryder stood up and turned around to offer Patty his hand. Patty smiled and shook hands then turned to leave, telling Jenny she would see her later.

'I must be going as well. It was interesting seeing you again, Jennifer.'

Helen shot away from her mother's side and grabbed Ryder's hand, her little face puckering with worry.

'But you have to stay with us now. Please,

Mummy, tell him he has to stay with us.'

She turned a begging face towards Jenny. Ryder looked down with a deep frown at the small figure clinging to his arm.

'This is where lies fail you,' he said, his voice harsh and accusing, then hunkering down to Helen's height he said in a much softer tone, 'I'll be back tomorrow.'

'But you don't have to live in a hotel now. You can stay with us, can't he, Mummy?'

'We don't have room here, baby.'

'You can have my bed.'

The small voice was so anxious that Jenny had to fight hard to keep the threatening tears at bay. Ryder was becoming increasingly uncomfortable with the situation so Jenny stepped forward and loosened Helen's grip.

'Say thank you for the lift and see you tomorrow, Helen,' Jenny said, picking her up into her arms.

But Helen's only response was to bury her head in her mother's shoulder and cry, as a scowling Ryder hurried to the door.

\*       \*       \*

Ryder returned the following evening with a bottle of wine for Jenny and a doll for Helen. The doll wasn't as big as Irma, Anna's doll, but it did something that Irma did not—it talked!

Jenny hadn't believed him when he said he would return, thinking it just an excuse to

32

pacify Helen. So she was taken aback when she opened the door an hour before Helen's bedtime to find him standing on the doorstep his arms full of presents.

Helen's welcome was rapturous and the doll the most wonderful toy ever invented. Jenny could see that the joy of telling Anna it was from her daddy would have made it wonderful even if it had been a rag doll with one eye missing. Because she had never expected Ryder to return she had delayed talking to Helen yet again.

Now, somehow, she was going to have to explain that although Ryder was her real daddy, he didn't believe that she was his daughter and that it was for the best to leave it that way.

She would tell her before he went back to America, then at least Ryder would be spared the embarrassment of her attentions in future. It was an impossible task and it turned the following two nights into restless nightmares for Jenny.

Ryder continued to visit until, on Friday evening when, almost as if Helen sensed something changing, she insisted that it was Ryder who put her to bed and read her a story.

'I leave tomorrow evening, so I won't be seeing you again,' he told Jenny after leaving Helen asleep. 'I admit I'll miss Helen. She's a lovely child and a credit to you.'

He was sitting across from her as they

sipped their wine.

'Have you no idea of the whereabouts of her father?'

'Oh, yes, I know where he is.'

He was watching her thoughtfully over the top of his wine glass. 'Then he doesn't have any idea what he's missing.'

'He doesn't want to know.'

'Are you sure?'

'Yes.'

He lowered his empty glass to the table.

'You were always such an impulsive, independent creature, Jennifer. Did you tell him?'

'No.'

'Then how do you know he will reject such a beautiful child?'

'He thinks me capable of sleeping around, thinks it could be someone else's.'

'I see, and do you sleep around?'

A sad, little twist curved the corners of Jennifer's mouth.

'What do you think?'

He shrugged and said nothing.

When he'd gone, Jenny gave her emotions full rein and sobbed until her head ached and pain sliced through her chest.

\*     \*     \*

'Please, if Mr Surtees hasn't checked out yet, will you get my message to him before he

34

leaves? It's very important.'

Jennifer replaced the receiver and pressed her clammy brow to the cool cream walls of the hospital corridor.

Helen's reaction when Jenny tried to explain the situation between herself and Ryder had been quietly accepted with screwed-up concentration. But the news that Ryder would no longer be coming to see them had caused a terrible crying scene. When it was over, Helen had relapsed into a dreadful silence which Patty assured Jenny would soften by the time she returned from a trip to the zoo.

An hour later, Patty phoned from the zoo to say that she was worried about Helen and was bringing her home. When they didn't arrive Jenny was in a terrible state imagining all sorts of catastrophes. Then the phone on the landing was ringing again and this time it was the International Hotel asking if she had a daughter by the name of Helen. When she agreed with them she was told there had been an accident and the little girl and her carer had been taken to the General Hospital.

*          *          *

Jenny moved back to the hospital waiting-room where Patty sat huddled in a corner.

'I don't understand,' Patty said, her voice full of tears. 'She was there by my side hanging on to my coat while I dug the bus tickets out of my bag. Then I looked down and she was gone. I asked everyone in the queue but nobody had seen her. I couldn't believe it. I'd been searching for a good fifteen minutes before I realised that the International Hotel was just across the road and remembered hearing you say that was where Mr Surtees was staying.'

Tears welled over and ran down her face. She pulled a large handkerchief out of her pocket and held it to her eyes.

'When I think of the wee one crossing that busy road and what could have happened!'

'Don't, Patty. You weren't at fault. I made a mess of trying to explain things to her. That's why she made a bolt for the hotel. Ryder said she might try to find him but I didn't believe him, and she crossed the road safely, didn't she?'

Patty nodded.

'Nobody could have foreseen that she would fall on those marble stairs and bang her head. If only they would come and tell us she's all right.'

The minutes ticked on and it was already half an hour since she'd made the call to the hotel. Had Ryder gone? Would he come if he got the message and risk missing his plane? A doctor was standing in the doorway. Patty had shot out of her seat before Jenny realised he was there. He spoke to Patty first but then she indicated that Jenny was the child's mother.

He smiled confidently.

'Helen will be fine, Mrs Carson. There's a hairline fracture which should heal well without too much bother at her age. Also several nasty bruises. The reason we shall be keeping her in is because she has yet to regain consciousness. This is causing us some concern. However, it isn't that unusual after such a nasty bump. Now if you would like to see her, nurse will take you up.'

He left the room after another quick smile and a nurse appeared in his place as if by magic.

Helen was in a small room by herself. Teddy bears pranced around the walls and bright yellow curtains half hid the light-defusing blinds. She looked so tiny lying flat and still under the pristine covers. Jenny caught her breath in her throat as she crossed the floor and sat down by her daughter's bed. Patty, after one look, pulled a chair up to the other side of the bed for herself.

At just that moment Ryder arrived looking angry and stunned at the same time. Patty rose to leave.

'I'll be back later,' she said to Jenny, patting her shoulder. 'I'll let Jack know what's happened. Is there anything you want me to bring back?'

Jenny tore her gaze away from Ryder and answered absentmindedly.

'No, not yet. We'll not know what's going to

happen until she wakes up.'

Patty left, closing the door quietly behind her.

'What happened?' Ryder demanded.

'She fell.'

'I know all that. What I mean is what was she doing at the hotel? Did you take her? Didn't you tell her I was leaving?'

'Yes, I told her.'

Jenny put a trembling hand out to stroke her daughter's brow.

'She seemed to accept it. Patty took her to the zoo to distract her but it didn't work and she ran away from Patty and went to look for you.'

She heard Ryder's drawn breath. He dropped into Patty's vacated chair and stared at the child in the bed.

'I should have quashed her ideas from the start. What on earth possessed you to let her have that old photo in the first place?'

'She found it in my drawer. She asked me if it was her father and because she was so desperate to believe in a father I let her.'

'I would have thought you would have destroyed all reminders of our marriage after I left.'

Jenny shrugged.

'I had to leave quickly at the time, or lose the opportunity altogether,' he went on. 'I left my contact number with Father. When you never rang I assumed you were no longer interested in our marriage.'

'We all make assumptions rightly or wrongly. At the moment my only thoughts are on my daughter, praying that she will open her eyes and recognise me.'

'Of course, I'm sorry. Is there anything I can do? Would you like a specialist to see her? I can arrange to have a private visit.'

'No, there's no need. The hospital will take good care of her. Anyway, I'm sure there's nothing anyone can do until she wakes up.'

Jenny laid her head on her arms and started to cry.

'It's too soon to give up now. Dry your eyes and we'll go to the restaurant and have something to eat. We might be here all night and we'll have to keep our strength up. You want to be bright-eyed and bushy-tailed when she does wake up, don't you?'

Jenny looked up astonished at his use of the plural.

'I'll stay on here myself.'

'No, you won't. You can do nothing here at the moment. You might as well do as I say.'

Reluctantly Jenny got to her feet.

'She might wake while I'm not here. She won't know where she is. She'll be frightened.'

'We'll tell the nurse at the desk on the way out and she'll send for us the minute there's any change. Now come on.'

He held out a hand to her and she allowed him to steer her from the room.

They were only away an hour before Jenny insisted on going back to the ward. When they arrived, Patty was sitting by the bed singing a nursery song in a soft voice.

'They said you'd gone for a break. There's not been a peep out of her but I've seen her eyelashes flutter a couple of times. Here, you speak to her,' she said, relinquishing her seat to Jenny.

Jenny sat down and took Helen's hand in her own.

'Mummy's here, darling. Helen, I'm here, please wake up. Oh, please wake up, baby.'

Ryder and Patty sat to one side as Jenny talked non-stop to the little girl. As time passed, her voice grew more and more desperate until Ryder moved forward and took hold of her shoulders. A nurse came into the room to check on her patient. Patty had told them about Helen's flickering eyelids but the nurse seemed unimpressed.

'It happens,' she said, taking the limp wrist in her hand and rubbing the inner surface with her thumb. 'It's only been a few hours. Try not to get too upset. She'll probably come round sometime during the night. It's just a matter of patience.'

'What time's your flight?'

Jenny looked round at Ryder. His skin tightened across high cheekbones.

'I won't leave until I know she's all right.'

Something inside Jenny relaxed. She turned

40

to Patty.

'Go home, Patty. I'll stay here overnight if you'll come back and relieve me in the morning.'

'Of course, love, anything I can do to help just give us a bell.'

'Thanks, Patty, and don't worry. I'm sure everything will be fine.'

She turned back to Helen when she heard Ryder say something and bend over the top of the bed.

Then she heard Helen say, 'Daddy,' and her heart leaped with pain.

## CHAPTER FOUR

Jenny watched Ryder striding angrily back and forth across the tiny sitting-room of her flat. The doctors had given Helen the all-clear and she would be home tomorrow. Ryder had promised the little girl he would be here for her when she came home but that hadn't stopped him being furious with Jenny for putting him in this impossible position.

'I thought you were going to tell her the truth,' he insisted.

'I did, but she's too young to understand. To her, the man in the photograph is her father. I told her we didn't live together any more but . . . '

He turned on her then.

'But you didn't tell her I wasn't and never had been her father.'

'How could I? She's loved you and dreamed about you all of her life.'

Jenny was angry now, too.

'And whose fault was that?' he insisted.

It was on the tip of her tongue to tell him everything but she was forestalled by the arrival of Patty.

'She's back to normal,' Patty said all in a rush. 'Gave me this list of things she wants brought in tomorrow 'specially to impress her daddy,' she said, giving Ryder a sidelong smile.

Ryder turned his back and went into the kitchen banging about with the kettle as Jenny took the list from Patty. She shrugged her shoulders at Patty's silent question. Then when the woman had left, she chewed her lip and glanced towards the now silent kitchen. He was standing in the doorway, a mug in each hand.

'I'll have to make some phone calls,' he said, handing her one of the mugs of coffee.

He was glancing round the room for the phone as he spoke.

'I don't have one. We share the one in the hall,' she said, anticipating his question.

'Don't tell me, it's a pay phone.'

She lifted her head in a defiant gesture.

'That's right.'

                    *        *        *

Jenny couldn't believe it—Ryder had taken a six-month lease on a flat in nearby Jesmond.

He called most afternoons and took Helen out. Patty was feeling decidedly rejected, and Jenny wasn't too happy about it either. If it hadn't been for the fact that she was now heavily into her finals and grateful for the spare time these visits afforded her, she might have been jealous of Helen's unbridled hero worship of her 'daddy'. As it was Jenny saw more of Tim than Ryder.

It was a shock to her one day when Tim, out of the blue, asked her to join him on a teaching job in Spain. She laughed at his outrageous idea.

'I can't drop everything and go off like you, Tim. What about Helen?'

'We take her with us. She'll love it, all that healthy sea and sun. It's only for the summer. A break we both deserve before we have to come back and concentrate on our futures. What do you say?'

Jenny sighed.

'It would be nice, wouldn't it, but what would I do with Helen during the day? Have you thought of that?'

He smiled, seeing her half persuaded.

'It's an infant school. She can sit in with you.'

Jenny laughed.

'You have it all worked out, don't you?'

'Yup.'

'I'll think about it.'

'Great, but don't take too long. I have to let them know.'

Jenny mentioned it to Helen that evening and was horrified when her daughter's eyes filled with tears.

'Is my daddy coming?'

'No. I've told you, we'll be with Uncle Tim.'

'I won't leave my daddy. Please, don't make me leave my daddy.'

Her voice was rising as she sobbed. Jenny had never seen her like this before.

'But, Helen, you love Uncle Tim. You know you do and Daddy has to go back to America some day.'

Helen was nodding her head and said on a hiccup, 'Take us with him.'

'What?'

'Daddy said we can go with him to America.'

I don't believe this, Jenny thought. How could he be so stupid as to make her a promise like that?

Jenny was so worried about Ryder's promise to Helen that she couldn't concentrate on the last exam of the finals and convinced herself that she had failed it.

Eight weeks of summer stretched ahead of her like a threat. She'd had no answer from the job applications she'd put out. The interview for the position she would really like was dependent on her results, so she wouldn't know about that until August.

Tim had been disappointed that she wouldn't be accompanying him to Spain. He'd suggested that perhaps Ryder was encouraging Helen's dependency on him as a way of getting back at Jenny for putting him in the rôle of father.

Jenny shook off this accusation as resentment on Tim's part and it wasn't until he'd been gone a week, and her expected time with her daughter failed to materialise, that Tim's suggestion returned to niggle at her.

Was it possible, she wondered, but look how angry he had been when faced with Helen's clinging behaviour before the accident. Had he become genuinely attached to her during the past few weeks. It wouldn't be surprising. She could be a little charmer when she wanted.

Have I made a mistake, Jenny wondered, allowing Ryder so much freedom with Helen.

*    *    *

She kept a close eye on them over the following days, accepting Ryder's invitation to join them on their trips to parks, museums and the zoo. This afternoon they were going swimming at the coast.

'There's waves and slides and a deep part that I'm not allowed to go in because Daddy says big people dive there and I might get hurt. I can dive, too, now, you know. Daddy showed me how. We didn't know it was there, did we, Mummy? We only went to the town baths and I was frightened of the noise, wasn't I?'

There hadn't been the money for trips to the coast, Jenny felt like justifying herself, as she bit her tongue. Ryder was, knowingly or unknowingly, undermining her relationship with her daughter. She would have to have it out with him next time they were alone.

The opportunity came sooner than she expected. They came home later than normal after eating out. Helen had fallen asleep in the car and Jenny was putting her straight into bed. Ryder was still sitting in the living-room watching the news on their small TV. As she came in he rose to his feet preparing to leave.

'Can you spare me a few minutes? There's something I want to say,' Jenny said.

'I have an important appointment at eight, but fire away. My career already hangs by a thread joining two continents.'

'Which is what I want to talk about.'

His eyebrows rose questioningly as he sat himself back down in the seat.

'I believe you've told Helen that you'll be taking her to America with you. Do you mind explaining to me why you made such a rash, impractical promise?'

'It was rather rash, I agree, but neither impractical nor impossible. Depends how we look at it.'

Jenny jumped up from her chair.

'What on earth are you talking about? We don't look at anything. I decide Helen's future. I'm her mother.'

'Calm down and sit down,' he snapped. 'What do you think I'm talking about here? Kidnapping? I was going to suggest that you both come back with me to America. You could get a good job out there and the kindergarten care is first class. I could continue to see Helen and in time she will stop being so possessive.'

Jenny sat back down with a thump.

'You have it all worked out, don't you? But you have overlooked one tiny thing, Ryder. I don't want to go to America. I love my daughter very much but I will not allow her to dictate my future.'

'You don't mind denying her her rights though, do you?'

His voice was cold with anger.

'How dare you!'

'I say it because she is just a baby with no-one to put her side of the argument against a mother who couldn't be bothered to inform her real father of her existence. I have work mounting up for my attention in America while I sit here baby-sitting someone else's child. You have nothing to hold you here and this,' he said casting a scathing glance around the room, 'is hardly the right environment in which to bring up a child.'

Jenny was so hurt and angry she dare not open her mouth. After a long, uncomfortable silence she rose once more to her feet indicating that she wanted him to leave.

He heaved himself out of his chair with an impatient sigh and gave her a long, hard stare before turning for the door.

'Please don't say anything more to Helen about America because I already have other plans for our future. Good-night.'

Her anger stayed with her while she did a quick tidy around. It was only nine o'clock and she couldn't settle to the television. There were plenty of other jobs she could be doing but the angry energy had gone leaving an empty sadness.

What would he do, she wondered, if he knew he was Helen's real father. He would be furious, but what would he actually do? What could he do? Would he apply for parental rights, have her branded as a bad mother? Her heart ran cold with the thought.

What were her rights? Could she stop him from taking Helen to America? Should she stop him when Helen was so attached to him? Would he have stayed with her if he'd known before he went to America? She didn't believe that was so.

She felt so afraid and alone standing before the window and staring out on to the empty street. For the last few years there had always been Patty or Tim to turn to when things were troubling her. Now she was on her own. She had turned down Tim's offer to go to Spain and Patty had withdrawn more and more since Ryder's arrival.

She stirred herself, feeling the chill seeping through her bones. He's right, she thought, gazing around her at the chipped furniture that no amount of polishing could hide. It was shabby.

You have two choices, she told herself in a firm voice as she went to make more tea. You can remain silent and go to America or you can tell him the truth and take the consequences.

On her way out of the kitchen she stopped by Helen's door. It was open a crack as it always was while she slept and Jenny opened it farther to creep across to the bedside and stand looking down at her daughter.

How could he not know, she marvelled for the countless time. In the early days she had searched avidly for some sign of herself in the tiny baby, catching only glimpses from time to time. Later, as Helen grew and became more like her father, Jenny had accepted her as Ryder's substitute and given her all the love and attention she might otherwise have shared with him.

She let go the heavy sigh from her chest and moved back into the living-room. The warm cup she cradled between her hands was placed down on the small table by the settee as she switched on the television and waited for the news. Suddenly he was there, filling the screen with a still photograph while the newscaster talked over it.

It took a while for Jenny's concentration to focus in on what the man was saying, something about a trip to the Amazon in the autumn. The picture changed to one of Ryder standing in front of a corrugated iron dwelling with two natives, one on either side of him. He was laughing at something the one on the left of him had said.

In seconds it was over and the newscaster moved on to other topics. But that stern face broken with laughter stayed with her, taking her back to days when they had both laughed at so many things and she had believed it would last for ever.

Reality was quite different though and now she must pay again for that dream.

\*      \*      \*

'We're going to America,' Helen sang as she danced around the kitchen table and through into the living-room.

Jenny tipped the uneaten toast into the bin and washed up the used cups and plates. Her decision had been made some time between dawn and Helen's arrival in her bedroom complaining of a sore tummy.

The sore tummy had miraculously disappeared and Jenny took her off to nursery after promising she could tell her friends that they were going to America. She did some shopping on the way home then called in to see Patty and warn her that they would be leaving and she would let her have the date when she knew it.

'I know you'll have to let the flat go but I hope you'll find a corner for us somewhere should things go wrong and we need it.'

She gave Patty a tremulous smile.

'Come on kind of sudden this, hasn't it?' Patty said.

Jenny nodded.

'He suggested it to Helen on a spur of the moment, not expecting that she would jump on it as gospel. We had an awful disagreement about it and I know I have always said that Helen would never be allowed to rule my life, but, well, we've drifted so far apart since Ryder arrived I'm afraid of losing her love.'

'Where did Helen get his picture in the first place? Was he an old boyfriend?'

Patty had never asked questions before and this one caught Jenny unawares.

'A long time ago, yes.'

'No chance I suppose that he could be the one—the father, I mean?'

Jenny was decidedly uncomfortable as she said, 'No, no chance at all.'

'Umm,' Patty said, 'just wondered. It would

51

explain a lot.'

'Explain what?'

'Well, you must admit there is a rather startling resemblance.'

'There are hundreds of men who look like Ryder.'

'It's not just his looks. Helen has similar mannerisms as well. Haven't you noticed the way she has of looking at you when she's cross? He looked at me exactly the same way the other night.'

'That's ridiculous! You're imagining things.'

'It's none of my business,' Patty said, 'but if there's the slightest chance that it's true then tell him because it's the only way you're going to get any peace of mind.'

Jenny sank into the nearest chair.

'If it's that obvious why hasn't he seen it?'

'We never see what's under our noses, love. People travel hundreds of miles for holidays they could have on their own doorstep if they stopped to look. Tell him, Jen. You might be surprised at his reaction.'

She left Patty's flat and made her way upstairs. By the time she had made herself some lunch and mulled over what Patty had said it was time to go and collect Helen. There was a children's event on at the Discovery Museum and Jenny had decided to take her there straight from nursery.

Margaret Mitchell was sitting in a blue saloon car at the nursery gates. She swung her legs from the expensive car and walked towards the nursery entrance alongside Jenny. Jenny continued to walk and spoke without looking at the other woman.

'I believe you might have a photograph belonging to me,' she said decisively.

'That's quite right. I was curious as to why your little girl might claim a friend of ours as her father. She referred several times to this photograph so I visited your apartment one day to ask to see it but you weren't in so the lady baby-sitting Helen asked me in. Helen gave me the photograph after I enquired about it. I meant to return it before I went to London, but you know how things are. I've actually brought it with me today.'

She handed it over wrapped in brown paper as they were filing into the large reception area of the nursery, where mothers, nannies and the odd father were claiming their children.

Jenny studied the tall, slim woman next to her and thought how skinny she was. The yellow heavy silk suit didn't go with her sallow complexion and a child had never been born with hair that tint of chestnut. The heavy gold and emerald jewellery was too much in Jenny's opinion for day-time wear. She was smiling at Jenny now as they moved forward to collect the girls.

'Daniel tells me it's all been terribly embarrassing for poor Ryder. They've been friends for years, you know, always confide in each other. I suppose you sent to the newspaper for his photograph and never expected to see him in the flesh. It must have been a dreadful shock for you when he turned up out of the blue like that. Of course, it's the kind of thing people like Ryder and Daniel have to cope with all the time.'

Horrified at the woman's suggestiveness Jenny pushed ahead and, taking Helen by the hand, hurried her from the hall as Margaret's voice called, 'Can I give you a lift?'


## CHAPTER FIVE

They flew from Newcastle to New York, and Jenny was feeling very proud of Helen's good behaviour during the long seven hours. She glanced across her daughter's sleeping form as Ryder returned to his seat by the aisle.

'We'll be landing shortly if you want to wake her and freshen up,' he said.

She woke the little girl with a gentle shake and after a minute or two they passed Ryder and made their way to the queue for the toilets. When they returned Helen was bouncing with energy once more.

'Isn't it exciting, Mummy? Soon we'll be seeing where Daddy lives.'

'Yes, dear.'

Jenny was shaking with nerves. Would they be met? How would they be travelling to Ridgefield? Would he dump them at this place he'd found for them without telling her how to go on? She couldn't even remember how many dollars there were to the pound. How was she to get around? Was there a good public transport system? All these questions were going around in her head when there was a thump and a screech as the undercarriage went down and the brakes were applied. They were on the ground shortly after.

Soon they had cleared Customs and were met at the entrance of the terminal building by a large bear of a man with a pleasant, open face and wide smile. He clapped Ryder on the back.

'Thanks for coming to meet us, Dan,' Ryder said.

'No problem.'

Together they loaded the baggage into the back of an estate car. Jenny who had been giving all her attention to Helen lost her concentration when she heard Ryder call the man Dan.

'Jennifer,' Ryder said, turning round to draw her forward, 'I don't think you've met Daniel Mitchell yet, Margaret's husband.'

'Hello. I thought you were still in England with your family,' Jenny said.

'Heck no, we all came over here last week. Didn't Margaret tell you? Why she's been so busy setting your apartment to rights she's had no time for anything else. I've been ordered to get you straight back so that you can rest up before meeting the others tonight.'

'The others?' Jenny frowned, not understanding, 'But I . . .'

The rest of her shocked enquiry was muffled as Ryder thrust her and Helen into the back seat and slammed the door. He climbed into the front passenger seat as Daniel started the engine and drove out and on to a wide highway. Their first impression of New York was depressing. Cracked concrete stuffed with weeds and graffiti everywhere. But after a while things improved. Jenny noticed detached houses with lots of green and many trees. Then as they travelled north there were miles of forest and groups of pretty, wooden houses. Large stores would suddenly appear out of nowhere set back from the road.

Helen was wide awake and exclaiming at everything, while Jenny stewed at the thought of Margaret Mitchell organising this get-together of strangers without as much as a by-your-leave. The dreadful woman must have packed up and left England only days after returning Ryder's photograph.

They had left home at six-forty-five that morning yet several hours later it was still midday in America. Ryder stopped answering Helen's interminable questions as Daniel boomed, 'Here we are, home, sweet home.'

He turned off the highway and up a narrow road that led into the forest. Through the trees Jenny could see the tops of dark yellow houses with balconies at various levels. Now long drives were leading off a wide sweep of roadway that encircled a large green with two beautiful wide spreading trees. The squeals from Helen were a joy to hear but Jenny's eyes had fastened on the white convertible and the tall, red-haired woman standing next to it waving excitedly.

The accommodation was the same two-bedroom, one public-room with bathroom and kitchen that she and Helen had shared in England but the generous size of the rooms and added extension of a balcony wide enough to eat on turned it into untold luxury. It was very hot outside and when Helen saw some other children gathered around what Ryder informed them was a communal swimming pool nothing would do but that she join them.

The Mitchells had gone, leaving the apartment full of flowers and groceries and promises from Ryder to bring Helen and herself over to their place that evening.

'Where is their place?' she asked Ryder as Helen disappeared into the bedroom.

'About twenty minutes' drive the other side of town.'

'I didn't see any town. Is it nearby?'

'About ten minutes by car.'

'But I don't have a car. What about this

57

school? Is that in the town?'

All her fears were being realised then Helen cried from the doorway, 'Mummy, I can't get the case open. The one with my things are in.'

'Is there any public transport?' she asked quite desperate now as she ignored her daughter.

Ryder was scowling at her, Jenny realised. He seemed to do little else these days. She was thoroughly sick of his constant disapproval. Who on earth did he think he was to uproot them like this then dump them and expect them to cope on their own? Feeling edgy and irritable she put it all down to the long journey and tried hard not to snap at him when he answered her.

'There will be transport, don't worry. But right now I'd say you need some rest and time to yourselves, to settle in. Margaret is a bit thoughtless at times but it's all well meant. I live on the top floor, by the way, and I'll pick you up at six.'

'Is this all your house, Daddy?'

Helen came tumbling into the room as he made to leave. He bent down to her level.

'Yes, it is, but I will be upstairs and you and your mummy will be downstairs.'

'Why? I want to be with you as well as Mummy.'

Jennifer watched the two faces so close together and felt the twist deep down in her heart.

'Helen, I've all ready explained that Mummy and Daddy don't live together any more. When you want to be with me you can come upstairs then when you want to be with Mummy, you can come downstairs.'

She quite liked this idea and with her head cocked to one side she asked, 'Will I have a bed upstairs and a bed downstairs?'

'Yes,' he replied as he stood up, stroking her hair thoughtfully.

Just for a minute Jenny held her breath, then it was over and he had gone.

\*      \*      \*

Laughter and music greeted them as they stepped out of the car. The house was ranch-style, long with a surrounding deck and a deep basement that looked out over the back yard. Ryder led them through the garage, up a short flight of steps and into a hallway that opened out into a large, wood-panelled lounge with a massive open, stone fireplace beautifully screened with flowers.

There was a bar at the far end of the room and patio windows leading outside. Helen had already caught a glimpse of her friend, Anna, outside in the garden and was straining to join her.

'Let her go,' Ryder said, 'and we'll find Dan and Margaret.'

Reluctantly Jenny let go of Helen's hand

and watched the little girl dash off to meet Anna. Together she and Ryder followed and within minutes were spotted by Margaret.

There were at least forty people in the garden, some prowling the edge of a large table set with food and drinks, others standing in small groups chatting and laughing. One or two were dancing under fairy lanterns hanging from the trees. And through it all a handful of children ran and shouted.

'Have a drink first,' Margaret said, crooking her finger at a passing waiter. 'Then you must come and meet the family.'

The waiter came and took their order and was back in a flash with their glasses balanced on a tray. Margaret guided them across the grass towards the group of people she had been talking to when they had arrived. Ryder immediately fell into conversation with Dan and it was Margaret who was left to introduce Jenny to the company.

'Jennifer, this is my brother-in-law, Wayne, and his wife, Sandra.'

Jenny smiled and offered a handshake to the overweight man with the bald head and his thin, pale wife.

'They have two boys running around here somewhere,' Margaret said giving a vague wave over the garden. 'Bobby and Darren.'

Time dribbled away and there were more names and more faces. She had lost track of Ryder at the beginning of the evening and only caught glimpses of him in conversation with different people as she was guided around the garden.

'She's from England, you know.'

The phrase was ringing through her head as she'd heard it repeatedly used about herself. Whatever it was meant to indicate attracted a multitude of questions every time it was said, and she heard herself answering them in the same repetitious style.

Jenny feared she wasn't coming over too well but to be honest she didn't really care. She was tired, she had a headache and all she wanted to do was crawl into bed. Helen was hyper by the time Ryder gathered them together and made their excuses to Margaret and Dan.

Jenny sat in the back seat of the car with Helen who by now was being really naughty and couldn't be trusted to behave herself. Ryder picked her up under one arm as they left the car and climbed the stairs to the apartment. About to pass her to Jenny as they stepped into the hallway, Helen was suddenly violently sick.

Ryder and Jenny stared at one another in surprise then back to Helen who was hic-cupping and wailing. Grabbing her daughter from Ryder's rigid grasp Jenny hurried her into the bathroom. When she came out again with Helen wrapped in a towel Ryder had mopped up the floor and was trying to clean the worst of it from his shoulder.

After putting the little girl to bed she came back into the living-room and offered to wash Ryder's shirt.

'Don't bother. It'll go into the service wash.'

Jenny was shaking her head.

'It's not like her to eat herself sick. Perhaps it was the combination of the long journey and everything else.'

Ryder eased himself away from the sink. The wet patches of his shirt were clinging to his body.

'From the smell, I would say it was alcohol.'

'What?' Jenny stared at him. 'My daughter wouldn't do anything like that.'

'No, but those two brats of Wayne's would.'

This was the last straw for Jenny and she erupted angrily.

'What have you done? You sneered at our home, went behind my back to promise my daughter she could come and live here, and she hasn't been here a full day and already she's been poisoned with alcohol. What kind of upbringing would you call this?'

Her voice had gradually risen until she now became aware that she was near screaming point. She stopped suddenly. Her head was threatening to split open and her chest heaved with every breath as she tried to calm herself. He raised a questioning eyebrow then turned and left.

In the morning there was an envelope slipped under the door. Inside was a note and an application for a driving licence. The questionnaire had been filled out and only her signature and photograph were required. The note said he'd call for it that evening when he would explain about her job and Helen's entry into the kindergarten. If there was anything else she needed he'd give her a lift down to the store.

Jenny bit her lip as she read. She was ashamed of her outburst the night before yet at the same time reluctant to accept that she would have to apologise to him that evening. Margaret Mitchell really had been generous with the food buying and Jenny was convinced that she wouldn't have to shop for at least a week.

Helen was much better this morning. After helping Jenny unpack their belongings and put them away she ate a little toast and fruit and slept for two hours although she had insisted she wasn't tired.

Later, she was splashing around in the swimming pool while Jenny lay on a lounger nearby, an open book alongside her. She wasn't reading. Her mind was spread out like feelers testing her new environment. She must make a list of all the questions she would ask Ryder when he came. Obviously he meant her to drive. She had signed the form and cut up a photograph to supply the picture required. But how much was all this costing? She couldn't be beholden to him. The independence she had struggled for must still be her ultimate aim.

It was six o'clock when he appeared. Helen had just finished her supper and was watching television before going to bed.

'Look, Daddy, I can watch cartoons whenever I like.'

She was curled up in the corner of the settee. Ryder sat down beside her. 'And what have you been doing today?'

'I've been swimming, haven't I, Mummy? And we met Christopher and Sally Ann and their mummy and grandma.'

He looked up at Jenny as she came through the kitchen doorway. 'They live across the green. Lenners, she said the name was.' He nodded.

'Yes, he's a pilot for a small firm over at Hartford.'

'They were very friendly. The little boy is a year older than Helen while the girl's not yet three. I'm making some dinner. Will you stay?'

A twist of a smile crossed his mouth.

'No, thanks. I had a heavy business lunch until three. By the way, you have an interview at the kindergarten next week, ten thirty on Tuesday, with a Mrs Doherty. Is there anything else you want to ask me?'

The amusement glittered in his eyes as she

brought out her list from the pocket of her jeans.

'First I need to know how much money all this is costing. I only have limited savings.'

A frown appeared between his brows as she continued.

'Secondly I need to know the running costs of this place, and how much it will be to send Helen to this kindergarten, also where I can buy a cheap car.'

By now Ryder was looking decidedly unsettled. He swept a hand through the fall of hair across his brow.

'This block of four apartments belongs to me. I lease out two and you and Helen are guests in this one. I shan't be looking for rent. As to your air fares, I brought you over on free air miles. A second-hand car won't be too much for your meagre savings and petrol is cheap here. I was going to offer to pay for Helen's schooling as it was my idea that you came here in the first place. You should have a generous salary from the school but if you find that you can't manage then I'll make you an allowance.'

Jenny was shaking her head.

'We don't want your money.'

'You didn't mind taking my father's money, though, did you?' he shot back.

Jenny felt the blood leave her face.

'That was different.'

'What's different about it. I'm still your

husband.'

Jenny's eyes flew to his.

'That's over and done with,' she whispered.

'Really?'

The scowl had left his face and his brows rose in question above hard grey eyes. Convinced he would hear the crazy rhythm of her heartbeat she rose to her feet and crossed the room.

'We are very grateful for this place but as soon as I get my driving licence and start work we'll be looking for somewhere else.'

'What? You haven't given much thought to Helen's feelings on the matter, yet again, have you?'

He left the doorway and came to stand behind her. She turned to face him her eyes blazing with all the turmoil of her emotions.

'How dare you talk to me like this! I love my daughter and until you came on to the scene we have always had a very good relationship.'

She tried desperately to control the sob in her voice.

'Now she seems to have swopped alliances, is that what you mean? And you resent it.'

'No.'

She was shaking her head angrily back and forth, her eyes on the tips of his highly-polished shoes. Then without knowing how or why she was in his arms, held close to his body her head tucked under his chin, one hand gently stroking her hair.

'Bow to the wind,' he whispered. 'Don't be so stubborn, Jenny.'

## CHAPTER SIX

The following Tuesday, Ryder took Jenny down to the kindergarten for her interview with Elaine Doherty. The headmistress was small, dark and not much older than Jenny herself. The woman's overall attitude, however, was friendly and Jenny left well satisfied that she could cope with anything that might come her way. The salary was generous, and Helen was to be allowed to stay on until Jenny was finished work after which they would travel home together.

Jenny had agreed to stay on at the apartment rent free and accept Ryder's offer to go fifty-fifty with Helen's nursery fees. Her driving test had been a great success and now she was on her way with Ryder's help to buy a second-hand car. The lot they chose was packed with every conceivable type of car. Jenny was staggered by the choice.

'How do we begin?' she asked Ryder.

'A simple matter of elimination.'

A greasy head appeared from beneath a truck not two yards from where they stood.

'You folks looking to buy?'

After some time and a few minor

67

disagreements, a small brown saloon was hers. Jenny was glowing with pride at her new acquisition when she drove home and stepped out, coming face to face with Margaret Mitchells' white convertible. She led Ryder into the apartment but there was no sign of Margaret.

'Perhaps she's upstairs,' Jenny said.

'Why should you think that?'

'Well, she let herself into my apartment before we arrived so presumably she has your key also.'

Ryder scowled as he replied, 'The estate agent has a set of spare keys for all the apartments. Margaret occasionally checks them out when I'm away.'

Jenny cast a quick look around.

'I wonder where she is then.'

'She probably came round, found we were out and has gone to visit a friend nearby. I believe Veronica Snider in the far corner is a particular friend of hers.'

'Can I get you something to drink? Helen's just discovered the ice-maker and we have enough to put icebergs in the swimming pool.'

'No thank you, I have work to be getting on with upstairs. Where is Helen, by the way?'

'Pam Lenners took her down to the pool with her own children.'

'I see. I'm glad you're making friends.'

She wouldn't have gone as far as that but before she could say so he had gone.

When Helen wasn't back an hour later, Jenny decided to wander down to the pool, and bring her back herself. But when she reached the poolside there was no-one there.

They'll be back at the Lenners' house, she told herself but Pam's face, when Jenny said she'd come for Helen, was a picture of horror.

'But I don't understand. Margaret Mitchell took her home for tea. She said she would give you a call as soon as you got back.'

Black rage filled Jenny's heart as she flew back across the green towards her apartment with only the briefest explanation to her neighbour. The phone was ringing as she entered. Jenny grabbed the phone from the wall and, forcing back the quiver in her voice snapped, 'Where's my daughter?'

'I haven't the faintest idea,' a bemused voice came back. 'Why, should I have? Isn't she back yet?'

Jenny swayed back on her heels.

'Ryder. That woman's taken her off without my permission. I thought that it was her I was talking to.'

There was a deep sigh at the other end.

'I suppose the woman in question is Margaret.'

'I'll have to go over there. She has no business . . . '

'All right. Look, give her a call first. You never know, she may well be on her way here and you'd look a bit silly passing each other on the road.'

As she replaced the phone it rang. Picking it up she recognised Margaret's voice immediately. Jenny charged straight in over the top of what Margaret was trying to say.

'How dare you take my daughter away without my knowledge!'

'She's been playing on Anna's new swing. When I saw her sitting there all on her own I felt so sorry for her.'

'She wasn't on her own. She was with the Lenners' children.'

'Well, she might have been with them, my dear, but Pammy and her male companion were doing their normal gossip thing and dear Helen was quite out of the way of the other children. I did call you but apparently you and Ryder had gone off somewhere so I left a message with Pammy and brought her home with Anna. Have you been back long? Is Ryder with you? My car was playing up again so I left it in your drive and borrowed a friend's. Ask Ryder to be a pet and see if he can get it going, will you? Otherwise he's going to have to give me a lift back home.'

'We've been home an hour and a half and Ryder is upstairs working. But I'll give him your message.'

'Great, we'll be over in a tick.'

And she rang off. Jenny continued to simmer until Ryder came downstairs.

'She's bringing Helen home,' and she gave

him Margaret's message.

'Wants me to fix her car, does she?'

His voice was so sharp edged she glanced up at him and caught the tic along his jaw. He's angry, she thought, as he disappeared outside and she heard him raise the garage door. But she was astounded twenty minutes later when he turned on Margaret with a sharp retort when she appeared with Helen and parked a blue car in Veronica's driveway and crossed the green to stand beside him.

Jenny whisked Helen off for bath and bed. On her return to the living area she overheard Ryder's angry voice as he told Margaret in no uncertain terms what he would do if she ever did anything like it again. Feeling rather elated by Ryder's support of her, Jenny reasoned that she had to be generous and forgive Margaret her high-handedness. But before she could do so she heard the car door slam and seconds later the roar of the convertible. Ryder and Jenny were left staring at one another across the room.

'It really wasn't necessary to be quite so hard on her. I suppose I did panic rather,' Jenny said.

'That has nothing to do with the matter. She knows the dangers perfectly well and should have been more thoughtful. Anna disappeared for two days when she was three years old. They were nearly out of their minds with worry. It turned out to be some young woman whose own child had died the day before. She hadn't made any attempt to cover her tracks and the police soon found her. It should have served to make Margaret think before doing such a silly thing. I can't imagine what she was thinking about.'

'Will you stay for a drink, something to eat perhaps?'

'I have a better idea. I have some brandy upstairs. After a fright like that I'd say you could do with a pick-me-up. I'll be back shortly.'

Jenny had placed two plates of ham, scrambled egg and toast on the glass-topped table by the time he returned. There were two small side salads and two glasses of white wine. From the corner of her eye she saw Ryder hesitate in the doorway, the bottle of brandy in his hand.

'I rustled up a bit of supper,' she said.

'Thank you. I don't keep much food in the apartment myself and going out for a meal when I'm busy with work at home is too much bother.'

'Well, sit down then. There's not much on offer, I'm afraid. I'm not into American food just yet. The idea of pancakes with everything hasn't quite taken off.'

He handed over the brandy and sat down at the table.

They ate in silence then Ryder said, 'Once I get this backlog of work cleared up I'll be moving around most of the time. Helen will soon get sick of the here-today-gone-tomorrow lifestyle I lead. Most women do.'

He spoke naturally and Jenny, eyeing him from beneath her lashes, wondered if that was the reason why he had never asked her for a divorce.

'I heard that you were going off to the Amazon in the autumn. Will you be away long?' she asked.

'It's difficult to say. There are always unexpected problems that can hold you up or even call the whole thing off if necessary. But we've planned for a six-week trip. I'll send photographs back to Helen when I can,' he said looking up and catching her watching him.

'Isn't it very dangerous?'

'There is a certain amount of danger but not as much as people think. The team all consists of professionals. We know and trust each other, that's the main thing. You can't go in there having to watch your back constantly in case some fool trips up.'

No, Jenny thought, and I'd hate to be the fool who did. They finished their meal and Ryder poured two glasses of brandy while Jenny stacked the dishes in the dishwasher. When she joined him again he was sitting in an armchair warming the brandy between his hands.

'Yours is on the dresser.'

She picked it up as she passed and moved to

sit in the chair opposite. They made small talk between sips of the warm brandy. Then Ryder put down his glass and stood up. Coming over to her chair he reached down and pulled her to her feet. Jenny stiffened, remembering that last unexpected kiss. But this time it was a mere peck on the cheek as he took his leave.

Helen christened their new car the Dude— one of several new words she had picked up since coming to live in the States. A great exam result had come through that morning from England and Jenny was itching to share her happiness with someone, but Ryder was in California and there was no-one else she felt close enough to for them to be interested.

They drove to the local store later that morning. Helen had great fun playing with the advertising toys scattered throughout the store, nibbling the various tasters offered and exclaiming at Jenny's inability to find any amounts small enough for two persons.

'We can't eat all that ourselves, Mummy.'

'We'll freeze it,' was Jenny's answer to everything.

When they were loaded up and ready to climb back into the car a voice hailed them from the exit of the store. It was Margaret. She turned to speak to the woman with her then ran over to where they stood. Jenny waited, wishing that she had just been that little bit quicker in leaving.

'My goodness,' Margaret cried when she

saw the car, 'is that the best Ryder could do for you? You mustn't let him palm you off with used vehicles. You never know what will go wrong with them.'

'Ryder didn't palm me off with anything. It's my car.'

'Well, I know but, anyway, thing is, I'm looking for helpers for Saturday evening, for a charity dinner and auction. I need six attractive women to lead the volunteer men to be auctioned on to the stage. I have four at the moment and am desperate for another two. Do say you'll help.'

'I'm afraid I can't possibly leave Helen on her own.'

'Good heavens, of course, you can't. Haven't you got hold of a good baby-sitting agency yet? Here take mine.'

She searched around in her purse and brought out a gold edged card with the name and telephone number of a local baby-sitting agency inscribed upon it.

'They're very good. Ask for Rita, she's real capable. Now, you won't let me down, will you? Ryder has already put up money.'

She gave a sly smile.

'Well, I suppose he couldn't volunteer himself, not when he was going to be in California,' she added.

Helen was trying to attract Jenny's attention from inside the car. 'I'm afraid I must be off,' Jenny said hurriedly.

'OK, don't forget now, seven-thirty sharp, Saturday, and wear your prettiest dress,' Margaret said as she walked away.

Jenny was grinding her teeth as she climbed in behind the steering-wheel, turned the key in the ignition and drove off.

'Mummy's going to leave me with a baby-sitter tomorrow night,' Helen told Ryder on the phone the following evening.

He always called her before bedtime when he was away, if at all possible. 'Helen!'

Jenny checked her daughter. She didn't want Ryder thinking it was a regular occurrence. She took over the receiver and spoke to him herself.

'Margaret has asked me to help at some charity function tomorrow night. I'm not happy about leaving Helen but I suppose I was steam-rollered into it, really.'

She heard his chuckle on the other end of the line and for an instant she closed her eyes and allowed herself to drift with the pain of remembrance.

'I wondered how long it would be before she raked you into one of her functions. Doesn't take no for an answer, does she? If you use the agency they use, Helen should be perfectly all right.'

'I suppose so but I shall make it perfectly clear to her that I won't be pulled into this sort of thing again. I don't mind donating to charity when I can afford it but I hate making a spectacle of myself.'

'It's all in a good cause, Jenny. Nobody takes it seriously.'

The humour was still in his voice when she retaliated rather sharply. 'I dare say but it didn't stop you buying your way out, did it?'

Then she handed the phone back to Helen, a little ashamed of her outburst.

Rita, the baby-sitter, arrived the next night with a form that Jenny had to sign. She was a nice girl, in her late teens, and Helen, who had stayed up to meet her, liked her on the spot. When Jenny left to drive to the Mitchells', the two of them were getting on great.

Jenny's heart was racing as she turned over in her mind what Margaret had said about what she wanted her to do—guide the volunteers on to the stage, wasn't that it? Well, that didn't sound too difficult. She didn't have a good dress but was wearing a long black skirt and glittery top of grey silver and various shades of red that she had kept for the odd occasion at college.

She'd sprayed the heels of her smart black court shoes once again and filled the small silver purse with her essentials. Her freshly-shampooed hair had shone under the bedroom lights as she applied the bare minimum of make-up.

The house was lit like a Christmas tree and Jenny had a hard job to find a parking place. At last she managed to squeeze in between two cars and left the Dude sitting there like the poor relation! With so many people there already she must be late but she distinctly remembered Margaret saying seven-thirty.

The meal was over and the staff clearing the tables when a maid took her coat and showed her into a small side room where five other girls were gathered. She was obviously no competition to them. The smallest of the girls came over to her and introduced herself.

'I'm Barbara Kleets. I haven't seen you around before.'

'Jennifer Carson. We only arrived here a few weeks ago.'

'Oh, my goodness, you're English.'

She turned back to the others.

'You haven't a chance tonight, girls, she's English.'

The remaining four girls surrounded Jenny and tossed one question after another at her about where she came from, why she'd come to the States, how long she'd known Margaret. Before she could answer there was a knock on the door and a man was standing in the opening, beckoning one of the girls.

'Oops, my turn. See you later, Jennifer.'

'Don't we all go in together?' Jenny asked.

A chorus of laughter greeted her.

'Gosh, no, she can only auction us one at a time.'

'Auction us? I don't understand. Margaret said we were to lead the male volunteers on to

78

the stage.'

Another burst of laughter followed this query and Jenny began to feel decidedly uncomfortable. If that dreadful woman had tricked her into coming here to take part in some caper then she was going to get more than she bargained for.

Barbara explained.

'Margaret auctions us on stage and the highest bidder has us for an evening out, that's all. It's good fun, especially if you get a real good looker. I got Jason Bellvidere last time. He's only eighty-nine!'

Jenny was horrified. Just wait until I get that woman on her own, she seethed. Jenny was kept waiting until last which added to the agony. When she walked out on to the stage she was anything but engaging. Her face was a mask of outrage though she cast a weak smile at the audience. Margaret blithely ignored Jenny's obvious hostility and started the bidding. It was rapid, much to Jenny's surprise, but eventually they all fell by the wayside as one man at the back of the room continued to outbid everyone else.

He was a tall man with sleek brown hair and film-star looks whom Margaret called Kane. The audience had fallen into a disquieting silence. Margaret bantered with them trying to encourage someone to stand up against Kane.

Suddenly there was movement at the back of the room and Kane was turning to acknowledge a newcomer from across the room, but Margaret brought down the hammer on Kane's offer and Jenny was handed over to him for an evening's entertainment.

## CHAPTER SEVEN

Ryder's features were carved from granite as he listened to Kane arranging to pick up Jenny the following evening. 'I thought you were in California?' Jenny asked.

She had never felt so relieved in her life as when she had spotted Ryder standing by the door at the back of the hall. Now, as her eyes searched his face, she wasn't so sure.

'You sounded nervous on the phone so I thought I would come back early to give you my support, though by the look of it you managed perfectly well without it.'

Jenny could have kicked his shins.

'I was terrified. Margaret tricked me, you know.'

One eyebrow raised in mocking disbelief as he said, 'Well, I dare say you won't be so terrified tomorrow night when I can't play chaperone.'

With her heart beating angrily Jenny contemplated a night out with the man she had met for the first that evening and of whom she

80

knew nothing at all. They left the house and made their way to their separate cars. Ryder moved off first and she followed him home.

When the sitter had left and Ryder had gone upstairs, Jenny looked in on Helen. The little girl was fast asleep, her favourite teddy tucked in alongside her. Back in the living-room, Jenny's thoughts turned to the shabby little flat back in Patty's house, and the days before Ryder's return into her life.

Where was Tim, she wondered. Was he still in Spain? She should have gone with him, she knew that now. Helen would have eventually recovered from her obsession with Ryder. Was she being strictly honest with herself, she wondered. Was Helen's obsession the only reason they were in America? Had she turned Tim down because there was the slightest chance that Ryder may have sometime in the future chosen to accept that Helen was his?

Had those days that she thought of as peaceful days before Ryder's reappearance really been so blissful or were they just empty, standing-still days, waiting for the time when Ryder would come back to claim her and their daughter.

The humidity was high that night. She was sticky and uncomfortable. Sleep was hard to come by. A shower beckoned. It was the tinkling of the wind chimes on the deck while she towelled herself dry that brought home the realisation that the patio doors were open. She pulled on the over-sized T-shirt she slept in and wandered through to shut the doors, frowning as she tried to remember when she had opened them.

As she turned back into the room she saw that both bedroom doors were wide open. She was already running as she slammed back Helen's door and searched with rising panic for her daughter. Back at the patio doors, she struggled with the locks, all fingers and thumbs now. Pushing them aside she ran out on to the deck.

The gate at the top of the steps was swinging open. Jenny called Helen's name as she hurried down them. A shadow slid across the lawn and disappeared into the edge of the woods. She called again, her heart pounding with fear, as she galloped across the gardens of the next block of apartments.

She found the path down to the swimming pool. Now the pool was in sight and Jenny called again in a voice as quiet and natural as she could make it. There was a splash and a squeal and Jenny saw three small heads seemingly floating on the surface of the water.

It was dusk and a wisp of grey mist lay along the edge of the forest surrounding the pool. Jenny's heart stilled, stopping the breath in her throat. Then she was running towards the water, tossing off her sandals as she went. Who was it in the water? Could she get them all out in time? Where was Helen? She closed her eyes and jumped.

Jenny's knees buckled beneath her as they absorbed the impact when her feet hit the bottom of the pool two feet beneath the water. She thrust out her arms to steady herself and gazed across the surface of the water from a kneeling position.

It was the ten-year-old twins from the next-door apartment and their eight-year-old sister who were swimming farther along the pool and now clung on to the edge, staring in astonishment at the strange spectacle of the English lady kneeling in the shallow end of the pool with a baggy T-shirt hanging beneath her.

Helen was curled up fast asleep in a lounger.

'We're looking out for her,' one of the twins shouted.

'Thank you,' Jenny called as she rung out her T-shirt and climbed out of the pool before picking up the grumbling Helen and carrying her home.

'I don't know how she got there,' Jenny was explaining to Ryder next morning as a sulky Helen had caught him on the way out and asked to go with him. 'She's never done anything like this before and now she knows she is never to sneak out again without telling me.'

Ryder glanced down at Helen then back at Jenny.

'I'm on my way to visit some very special

children today. It's a school for disabled children and they are running out of funds. We're going to do a documentary on facilities for disabled children and their funding when I return from the Amazon. This is just a run-up visit to meet the people involved. I think Helen might enjoy the experience and it will give you plenty of time to prepare for your date tonight.'

Jenny pursed her lips at his suggestive tone, but it would be a relief to have a day without Helen.

'By the way, do you have a sitter for tonight?' he added.

Jenny's hand flew to her mouth.

'No, I forgot, probably because I was hoping something would happen to make it impossible for me to go.'

'Oh, heaven forbid that should happen. I'll baby-sit. She can sleep upstairs tonight. How about trying out your other bed?' he said to Helen who was dancing around with glee.

'Can I, Mummy? Can I really? You promised. You said I could sleep in any bed I wanted.'

They left together, Helen prattling away non-stop. Jenny smiled. It was wonderful having the whole day to herself. Much as she loved her daughter, it could be tiring coping with the never-ending questions and demands for attention. She basked in idleness. She washed and curled her hair a new way, read a book while lying in a perfumed bath, gave herself a manicure and pedicure and painted her nails. It was all great fun though, she felt, not quite her style.

By the time Ryder and Helen came home she had prepared a light meal for three, after which Helen proclaimed that she would go upstairs with Daddy.

Left alone once more Jenny tidied up then moved into the bedroom to add the last touches to her make-up and slip into the black skirt, with a different top this time. By eight o'clock she was as ready as she would ever be, perched on the arm of the chair. She had never been on a blind date before and wasn't looking forward to the experience. With two minutes to go, there was a sharp rap on the door. Jenny fixed a smile on her face and walking forward, opened it. Ryder stood there. His expression was forbidding. With a sigh she dropped her arm and allowed him to enter.

'For heaven's sake, what have you done to yourself? You look like a tart.'

'How dare you talk to me like that!' Jenny snapped.

'Because you don't know what you are doing encouraging a man like Kane Gleason.'

'I am not encouraging him!'

'Looking like that you would give any man the come-on.'

Jenny glared back at him, a retort trembling on her lips as the doorbell went a second time.

She pushed past Ryder to answer it. This time it was her date for the evening, looking very smart in evening wear with a gift box in his hand. He smiled broadly as he eyed Ryder.

'I didn't know you already had company,' he said, tongue in cheek, 'or I would have ordered a table for three.'

Ryder froze him out with an icy stare then with one last scathing look at Jenny he was gone.

'Surly, isn't he? But we won't let him spoil tonight, will we?'

The open grin was there again as he handed her a beautifully-wrapped box of chocolates then offered his arm. It set the tone for the night and Jenny relaxed in the experienced aura of Kane's charm.

They dined in the front room of a pretty clapboard house. A notice and arrow announced museum and antiques towards the back of the house. Kane informed her that it was very difficult to obtain a table in the restaurant, for the food was first rate, the service good and with only fifty the tables were in constant demand.

Their table was set in the paned bay window that looked out across a small veranda hung with masses of flower baskets and tubs on to the street. Jenny gazed with interest at all the samplers on the walls and the rag mats beneath their feet.

One large wall was covered in a beautiful

quilt of creams and blues, its design picked out in the many patterned squares.

Kane was delightful company if a bit predictable in his gentle flirting. When, after a wonderful meal, he suggested a drive to a local beauty spot, Jenny turned him down making Helen her excuse. She could tell he wasn't very pleased but reluctantly he agreed to take her home. When he parked the car outside her apartment the smile was back on his face and he shrugged his shoulders.

'To have been in such charming company was worth every dollar,' he said.

Jenny hesitated as she was about to step out of the car. She felt guilty for he had paid an enormous amount of money for the privilege of taking her out and she guessed he was feeling short-changed. Quickly she leaned over and kissed him on the cheek.

'May I see you again?' he called after her as she stood on the street.

'Well, I don't usually . . .'

'I'll call you.'

Several days passed after her date with Kane. He rang twice asking her out, but she refused each time, making up a different excuse. Now, out of the blue, Margaret had rung to invite her and Helen over for brunch, squealing over the phone that she had no idea that Jenny and Ryder had once been married. How had she found out, Jenny wondered. Had Ryder told her? If so why, when he had kept quiet about their marriage all this time? Reluctantly she had promised to go, but she would be on her guard for she no longer trusted the other woman if in fact she ever had.

*     *     *

They arrived in brilliant sunshine at the hottest time of the day. Jenny was already damp and uncomfortable as they were shown to parasol-shaded tables on the back deck. There were some half a dozen people seated at the tables and several children seated on the floor of the lounge watching television.

Helen went straight off to join the children while Margaret came across to welcome Jenny. She was seated at the table and introduced to the company there and offered a salad and a glass of something to drink.

'You are a sly thing keeping your marriage a secret, you know. We all thought, well, you know.'

She shrugged her shoulders and cast a quick glance around her friends' faces.

'Ryder explained that you had been separated but were now back together again,' she said and smiled benignly.

Jenny smiled back and proceeded to eat her salad, offering no explanation.

'I suppose one apartment was too small for the three of you. Ryder did mention that he needed the extra space to work in. Of course when there is a child in the house the husbands always need somewhere for peace and quiet.'

Jenny took a gulp at the drink in the tall glass. She hadn't a clue what it was but it was refreshing. Helen appeared just then, in tears. She had fallen out with Anna and the little boy next to her had punched her. She cuddled into Jenny's skirt.

'Of course, her likeness to Ryder was obvious to me right from the start,' Margaret informed her guests.

Jenny clenched her teeth and smiled, while trying surreptitiously to stop Helen from chewing the bottom of her tunic. It was a nervous habit she had developed as soon as she could walk. She clung to Jenny's leg. Jenny glanced questioningly at her daughter for it had been sometime since she had last indulged in this type of behaviour. She stopped eating and, picking the little girl up, sat her on her knee. But Helen only buried her face in Jenny's bodice.

'I hope you don't mind, will Friday do?'

Margaret was talking to her again and she had missed what was said.

'Sorry?' Jenny said, as she continued to try to settle Helen.

'Shopping,' Margaret repeated, casting a patient glance around her friends. 'Would you be free on Friday to go shopping?'

'Yes, yes, I'm sure that would be all right,' Jenny replied, too distracted by Helen's behaviour to worry about Margaret and a shopping trip.

She made her excuses and left shortly afterwards. Her hostess was rather put out but smiled knowingly when Jenny explained that she was worried about Helen.

'Of course,' she said. 'I'll give you a ring later to check how she is.'

Once home Jenny sat Helen on a chair and, kneeling beside her, stroked the dark hair back from a hot forehead.

'Are you going to tell me what's wrong. Do you feel ill?'

Helen shook her head.

'Did the little boy hurt you when he punched you?'

Another shake of the head.

'Did Anna upset you?'

This time the little head nodded up and down and tears trembled on her lashes. Jenny's brow creased into a frown.

'What did she say?'

Helen's lips quivered, her head dropped and she spoke so softly that at first Jenny couldn't believe what she was hearing.

'Anna said my daddy didn't want me 'cos I was igitamate. What's igitamate?'

Jenny's fury rose in her throat and she fought to conceal it as she hugged the little girl close.

90

'It's all lies. Don't believe a word she says.'

Helen hiccuped a couple of times then leaned back and gazed into Jenny's face.

'You told me Daddy was mine but that he didn't believe you so we had to keep it secret.'

Jenny stared into her daughter's big, pansy eyes. Was this what the old saying meant when it said that your words could come back to haunt you? Jenny took the two podgy, little hands with their curled fingers and sucked thumb and carefully straightened them out and placed them together within her own.

'Daddy loves you, Helen. He was away from us a long time. You came along after he left and he didn't know about you. Mummy and Daddy had fallen out, you see. So when he came back . . . '

' 'Cos I found him.'

'Because you found him. He didn't know where you had come from or whose little girl you were. So we have to wait until he remembers.'

'Hasn't he remembered yet?' she asked gently.

'Not yet, sweetheart, but he will soon. He is your real daddy and you can tell Anna I said so.'

Long after Helen had gone to bed, Jenny waited for the sound of Ryder's return, determined to tell him the truth once and for all. If he didn't believe her then it was his loss.

# CHAPTER EIGHT

It was two o'clock in the morning before Jenny remembered that Ryder was in New York for the next three nights. She had only just fallen asleep when the telephone rang. Barely awake, she picked up the receiver and mumbled her name.

'Hello, may I speak to a Mrs Ryder Surtees, please?'

Jenny was wide awake now and struggling in bed to ask, 'Who wants her?'

'This is Danbury Hospital and I've been given this contact number for a next of kin.'

Jenny's heart thudded.

'That's all right, I'm Mrs Surtees. Carson's my maiden name.'

'Mrs Ryder Surtees?'

'Yes.'

'I'm afraid your husband's been injured in a traffic accident. His injuries are superficial as far as we can tell but he has yet to regain consciousness.'

'I'll be there as soon as I can,' Jenny replied immediately.

'He's being assessed now. The doctor will be available to explain the situation to you when you arrive.'

Jenny was silent for several seconds as she tried to assimilate what the nurse was saying.

Then she thanked her and replaced the phone. Her panic was already subsiding and her mind clearing. One thing at a time, she scolded herself. But her heart was racing. How ill was Ryder? Could she find this hospital on her own? What did she do with Helen?

Getting to the hospital was her first priority. No, she checked herself, first get washed and dressed, then wrap up Helen and get her into the car. With Helen settled comfortably on the back seat, Jenny climbed into the driving seat and turned the key in the ignition. There was a horrible whining sound, then a splutter and nothing. She turned off the key, sat back, and took a deep breath and tried again. Same thing happened.

Conscious of her sleeping neighbours and anger at the engine for failing her in this hour of need, she tried coaxing the engine with a gentler touch. The noise was louder than ever and had Helen awake and hanging over the back of the passenger seat wanting to know what they were doing in the dark.

Thoroughly fed-up and afraid of what was happening at the hospital, Jenny climbed back out of the car and with Helen held close, went back into the house. She placed Helen on the settee then picked up the phone and rang Margaret Mitchells' number. It was the middle of the night and Margaret wouldn't be happy at being disturbed, but what else could she do?

She was right, as she listened to the other

woman grumbling on the end of the line. But once Jenny explained what had happened there was a short screech then a garbled, 'We'll be with you shortly,' and the phone went dead.

It was Dan who arrived with the offer of a lift to the hospital while Margaret was to stay and keep an eye on Helen who had been put back to bed but was still awake. Their offer of help was generous and genuine and Margaret's spontaneous behaviour showed a new side to the woman who constantly irritated Jenny.

Dan quizzed her on the way to the hospital.

'Did they say how bad it was?'

'No, the nurse I spoke to said the doctor will tell us when we get there. I don't understand what he was doing on his way back so soon. He was supposed to be staying in New York until Friday.'

She could hear the worry in Dan's voice as he told her that Ryder had rung the office to say that he had finished the interviews sooner than expected and was on his way home. She didn't fail to notice that Ryder hadn't deemed it necessary to ring her with the news of his early return.

The hospital visit lasted only a short while, but the sight of Ryder suddenly so vulnerable in his stillness had shocked both of them. The doctor had spoken to them for several minutes explaining that until he regained consciousness, it was impossible to say what damage he had sustained.

'Once he does and we have assessed that there is no damage, then he will be fine. In the meantime all we can do is wait.'

On their return journey, Jenny glanced across at Dan's profile in the light from the dashboard. His chin was rough and his hair looked to have been raked through with his fingers instead of combed. Altogether he gave the impression of a large, disreputable teddy bear just awakened from hibernation. His mouth had turned down and his nostrils flared for a second before he spoke.

'Margaret said there had been a separation with you and Ryder. Must have been a long one. In five years, he never mentioned having a wife.' The remark hurt Jenny.

'He wanted to come to America, I didn't, so we went our own ways,' she explained.

'Helen's five, isn't she? I'm amazed he didn't want to stay for her sake. He loves children, can't do enough for them. But you're right, he's always loved his job. Pity you didn't come back then. He's been a new man since you and Helen came over.'

Jenny attempted to interrupt him but he shook his head.

'It's true he never stops talking about you both. It doesn't take a psychologist to see that you're what's been missing in his life. And if that stricken look at the hospital was anything to go by, you love him, too, honey, so what's the problem?'

Jenny was feeling light-headed.

'He won't accept that Helen is his.'

Putting the truth into words released a great dam of relief. Silent sobs wracked her body. Dan drew the car to the side of the deserted road and stopped then pulled her into his warm embrace. In time, she was still and he withdrew his hold. Dry-eyed, she stared out into the darkness and in a quiet voice told Dan what had happened since Helen had claimed Ryder as her daddy.

'And you never told him the true facts?'

Jenny shrugged.

'He wouldn't have believed me.'

'You don't know that, honey. He at least has the right to decide for himself. He's going to be pretty mad when he finds out. You are going to tell him, aren't you?'

Jenny's eyes swung slowly across to the reflection of her face in the windscreen. She'd made a silent promise to Ryder as she'd watched his unconscious face on the stiff white pillowcase and remembered his care of them. When he recovered she would tell him the truth, that Helen was his. What he did after that would be up to him.

'Yes, I'm going to tell him,' she said quietly.

Four days later, unknown to anyone, Ryder dismissed himself from hospital. Jenny knew nothing about it. She had been visiting the hospital mornings and evenings, leaving Helen with Margaret's nanny. Margaret had insisted on coming along with her the first time but as soon as Ryder regained consciousness, Margaret found a prior engagement.

Jenny had just returned from dropping Helen off before her morning visit to the hospital when she head the thump from Ryder's apartment. Quietly she crept upstairs and listened at the door. All was silent. Jenny cast a quick look around her. If either of the two neighbours on the opposite side of the stairs saw her, heaven knew what gossip they would spread around the estate.

It was as she turned away that she heard the phone ring. Expecting it to continue unanswered she ignored it. When it stopped and she heard the low tone of someone answer it, she ran back up the stairs and knocked on the door. If the person inside was an intruder she wasn't quite sure what she would do. On the other hand, she couldn't imagine a burglar answering a telephone!

There was a further silence and Jenny waited with baited breath for someone to open the door. She knocked again, harder than before. She heard the lock being disengaged and the door was flung open.

'What has a person to do around here to get any peace?'

Jenny stepped back, shocked.

'What are you doing here?'

'I live here. What do you want?' Ryder snapped, to Jenny's dismay.

'Why have you left the hospital? I was just going over there. They haven't let you out. The doctor said it was too early.'

'It was a hospital not a prison. I'm free to leave.'

He was standing in the doorway, his hair tousled. A livid bruise was visible at the height of its discoloration, from brow to just below his right ear. He wore a white bath robe tied loosely at the waist, his feet were bare and in his hand he held a towel. He moved back into the hallway when it became obvious that she was not to be dismissed easily.

'They don't make a very good job of washing you in there and I couldn't wait to get all the muck off.'

'That's because they concentrated on your wounds first. If you'd stayed long enough they would have bathed you thoroughly.'

She went through into the bathroom without waiting for permission. There was dirty water in the handbasin and a limp towel hung over the bath. On the floor lay a pile of torn, dirty clothes spilling from a plastic carrier bag. She moved back into the living-room.

'What were you trying to do in there?'

He had eased himself down on to the arm of the nearest chair. With an impatient sigh he said, 'I was side-swiped. The car rolled off the road and down an embankment. My head smashed the side window on the way down, then a tree stopped the roll and I ended up on the edge of a river, half in half out of the water. I must have been unconscious for some time. When I came to and tried to get out, a piece of metal nicked my leg. I got filthy dirty. They cleaned and wrapped up the leg, patched up the head, but I don't feel I've been washed thoroughly. When you demanded entry just now, I was about to cover my leg dressing with a plastic sheet to keep it dry while I had a shower and washed my hair.'

'I can do that for you,' she offered, hoping to get the chance to say what she had been trying to tell him since his recovery.

He jerked himself upright.

'There's no need. If you'll just take yourself off I'm quite capable.'

Jenny took a deep breath.

'There's something I have to tell you. I haven't been able to with Margaret being with me when you woke up and now you discharging yourself so soon.'

He was crossing to the bathroom and she followed in his wake, talking to his back.

'Keep it until later,' he said, closing the bathroom door in her face.

Jenny let herself out and moved slowly down the stairs back to her own apartment. Her promise to him when she thought he was going to die stuck like a knot in her throat.

That evening Kane phoned to ask her to accompany him to a small business dinner. His secretary had been called home on a family emergency and it would look bad for him to turn up without a partner. He was very solicitous when hearing about Ryder's accident and agreed it was a shame that he would be unable to sit with Helen. However, he had his own recommendation for that problem in the shape of a niece who was staying with him at the moment. Trapped, Jenny had no choice other than to be downright rude or agree and go with him.

'The meal won't take long,' he said when they were driving to the restaurant where the meeting was to take place. 'Then we can go on to a club or do whatever you'd like to do.'

The niece he'd introduced as Diana was a tall, leggy seventeen-year-old who had arrived loaded down with study books. She'd seemed pleasant enough but Jenny wasn't happy at leaving someone she didn't know in charge of Helen.

Her unease was still in the back of her mind as she said, 'Thank you, but I would still prefer that we go straight home after the meal.'

'I can't let you do that. You're doing me a great favour by sitting in for this meal. You must at least let me buy you a drink afterwards.'

'Well, perhaps only one.'

Jenny groaned inwardly while still managing to smile.

The restaurant turned out to be a large, wooden building on the edge of the forest with a salon bar front and a steeply-sloping garden at the back. Tables and chairs were set out on the wide, beflowered deck overlooking the semi-wild garden with its fast-flowing river along the bottom. The company made up three couples. A large, heavy man with a drinker's nose and his tiny wife whose eyes darted everywhere but at the person speaking to her; a couple in their thirties, both tall and slim, with a fashionable, healthy look; the third couple was middle-aged, clean and tidy but fashion had passed them by.

It was a strange mixture for no-one around the table seemed to know anyone else and if business was discussed then it must have been in some sort of code, Jenny decided. Kane was correct in promising a short meal, for though the food was first rate and the men well replenished, every member of that strange group appeared ready to leave at the first opportunity.

The drive up state had taken them forty minutes and for the first fifteen minutes of their return journey Jenny relaxed in a comfortable silence. It was dark now so it was some time before she realised that they were not returning by the same route.

'Didn't we come up route forty-seven?' she asked.

'Yes, how silly of me not to explain. By taking this alternative route we'll enter the opposite end of town and stop off for that drink I promised you.'

The white two-story building they stopped in front of looked more like a family house than a drinking place. She recognised the late-night store on the opposite side of the road so knew with some relief that they were at least on home ground. What she wasn't expecting was the difficulty she had in persuading Kane that she just wanted to get home.

She wasn't panicking exactly but she knew she was totally dependant on Kane for a lift. It wasn't the kind of place where she could hail a taxi or walk home from, for there was often gaps of several miles between one part of town and the next.

She was trying to disengage her hand from Kane's when she glanced over his bowed head as he kissed her palm, and through the window saw a familiar car enter the well-lit parking lot. Surely not! She bit down hard on her lower lip as she watched Ryder climb awkwardly from the car and begin to cover the ground towards them. With a hasty apology to a shocked Kane she picked up her bag and dashed from the car. Ryder was only yards away when she blocked his path.

'I'm so glad I bumped into you. Could you give me a ride home, please?' she said quickly.

A nerve flinched along his jaw as he studied her face in the overhead lighting.

'What about your friend? Shouldn't you tell him you're going?'

102

'I have. I explained that I was tired.'

He limped forward, his hands clenched at his sides. Then, taking her by the arm, he marched her across to his car.

'Don't do that,' she ground out, shaking loose his grip. 'What are you doing out here anyway?'

She was on the point of climbing into the car when he said, 'Chasing after you, as usual.'

'What?'

'The kid downstairs knocked me up. She said it was late and her boyfriend had come to give her a lift home, so could I see to Helen for her. She said I needn't come down if I would just listen out for her. You must have been desperate to go out, to go and leave Helen in such irresponsible hands.'

He had turned on the engine and was reversing out of the carpark. Jenny was livid.

'How was I to know she would do a thing like that and come to that, where is Helen? If you've left her alone I'll . . . '

'I put the fear of the devil on the girl and told her to stay where she was until I got back.'

Jenny could have strangled Kane and his niece, but her rage at Ryder was totally unfocused. He was determined to misunderstand every single thing she did and that hurt.

If she tried to explain about the business dinner she knew he would twist it into something it wasn't and she would end up looking more like a wicked, uncaring mother than ever.


## CHAPTER NINE

Back at the apartment, Ryder quickly paid off the sitter and showed her and her boyfriend the door. Jenny looked in on Helen who was fast asleep. An empty dish of ice cream on the bedside table and sticky papers scattered across the quilt indicated the need for bribery. Jenny shuddered, picked up the rubbish and empty dish and left the room.

Ryder was standing in front of the fire recess. His features were rigid and Jenny, after one swift glance, ground her teeth and marched into the kitchen. He followed her across the room.

'Did you do this sort of thing in England?'

Jenny placed the dish in the sink and swung round to face him.

'Did I do what sort of thing in England?'

She felt the hot blood of anger rise up then fall away from her face, leaving her icy cold.

'Leave Helen with strangers when you went dating.'

'I never did any dating as you call it and if I had to go out at all, Patty took care of her.'

His eyebrows lifted in an unbelieving expression as he turned to leave. Jenny crossed the floor behind him and sat down in a chair. She was weary and sick at heart at the sneering rejection she knew she would receive from him when she told him of Helen's birth. But she had made herself a promise and she could delay telling him no longer.

'Please don't leave. There is something you have to know. Something I must tell you.'

He was slow in turning back, almost as though he already knew what she was about to say. His brows pulled down in a frown as he accepted her invitation to sit in the chair opposite. Jenny took a deep breath.

'Helen accepts you as her father, Ryder, because you are her father. I was eight weeks pregnant when you left for America. Your father supported me through college because he knew Helen was his grandchild. He agreed to withhold the information from you because we both felt that it would hinder your future ambitions.'

The deathly silence which greeted her words was broken by a long hiss from Ryder's throat. He'd lost what little colour he had as she spoke. She waited, eyes fixed on the top button of his jacket, for the disbelief, denial, denouncement. It never came. Instead, he rose to his feet and left the room without a word.

\*     \*     \*

It was two days before she heard anything

from him other than his footsteps down the stairs or the slam of a car door. She interpreted his silence as disbelief of her story and by the third day she had other things to worry her.

They were well into September now and Jenny was enjoying her work at the school. The school bus would pick Helen up at eight-forty-five, then Jenny would drive down and prepare her class of seven-year-olds for the day. Helen would come in at three thirty and stay with Jenny until she was finished work then they would travel home together.

Today Helen was in a grizzly mood and refused to go out to the school bus.

'I want to go with you, Mummy,' she repeated several times and burst into tears.

This wasn't like her at all and Jenny worried that she might be sickening for something, so she gave in and took her daughter with her.

It wasn't until later in the day that Helen's teacher took Jenny aside and suggested that she thought Helen may be the victim of name calling or teasing and perhaps this was what had upset her.

Jenny talked to Helen that evening before putting her to bed. It turned out that she and Anna had fallen out.

'She was saying nasty things about you, Mummy.'

Jenny comforted her as best she could.

'Don't worry, sweetheart. She'll soon forget

and then you will be friends again.'

'No, I won't. I don't ever want to be her friend again.'

Jenny didn't blame Margaret's daughter because she was well aware of what a little copy-cat the child was and knew she would only be repeating things she had heard in her mother's company. Jenny was reluctant to tackle Margaret about the problem and hoped it would solve itself over the weekend.

It was a horrible shock on Monday when Helen was brought to the nursery by her teacher, with a large bump on her head and a tear-stained face. Jenny's first reaction was that Anna Mitchell had attacked her daughter. Then the shock really took hold when the teacher explained that Helen had been the guilty party.

Jenny talked to her daughter again that evening. Helen hung her head but refused to reply and went off to bed without supper. The following morning she refused point blank to go to school. There were screams and tears and eventually she fled upstairs to Ryder's door and sat sobbing in his doorstep. Jenny was on the point of picking Helen up when the door was flung open and Ryder, taking one swift glance at what was going on, swooped down and enfolded the weeping child into his arms.

'You had better come in,' he called over his shoulder to Jenny as he marched down the hall with Helen.

Jenny, angry at being put in this position by her daughter, moved down the hall and stood watching from the doorway as Ryder rocked the child back and forward as she sniffled into his shoulder. There was a suitcase and haversack standing against the living-room wall. Jenny's eyes shot back to Ryder. Was he leaving for the Amazon already without a word to either of them?

They hadn't spoken to each other since the night she had revealed the truth to him about Helen. It seemed to her as though he was denying ever having been told.

Helen's sobs eased and she wriggled to get down. Ryder sat down in the nearest chair and took her on to his knee. His face was close to her chubby, flushed one as he spoke.

'What is it, baby?'

Helen's eyes slid over to Jenny then up to her father.

'Why don't you want me, Daddy?'

Jenny closed her eyes. Ryder's face had turned to stone.

'Who says I don't want you?'

'Mummy says you are my daddy but you don't believe that I'm your little girl and we have to wait until you do.'

His icy glare pinned Jenny. Over the little girl's head his mouth screwed hatred and Jenny, feeling the pain and fear curdling in her stomach, dashed for the bathroom as it swirled up her throat. She wasn't aware of his answers to Helen's questions but when she came back out of the bathroom Helen left with her quietly.

Back in the apartment, Helen went straight to her room and closed the door, something she had never done before. Deciding that her daughter needed her own company, Jenny let her be and phoned the school to say that she and Helen were both feeling under the weather and wouldn't be coming in that day.

In the days that followed, a subdued Helen agreed to accompany Jenny to school where she was allowed to stay quietly in her mother's class. Margaret had rung with another offer of a shopping trip but Jenny had declined on the grounds that she couldn't leave Helen at the moment. Margaret followed Jenny's rebuff with a lecture on the dangers of pampering children and Jenny had to bite her tongue very hard not to point out that many of Helen's problems had started with Margaret's own daughter.

A letter arrived from Patty to say that Tom was back from Spain and had called in to see her and to ask about Jenny. On its heels came one from Tom himself. He appeared to have forgiven her for her rejection of his summer holiday suggestion. The spell in Spain had been a great success, and there was an offer of a permanent teaching post should he want it. There were several pages of the fun and laughter he had shared with new friends and descriptions of new places and the impressions he had gained from them.

He asked about her new life and after Helen. The writing had blurred as she came to the end of the letter. It took her a minute or two to realise that the blurring was because her eyes were full of unshed tears.

She read the funny parts of the letters out to Helen who was starting to read quite well. Then the little girl handed over her own letter for Jenny to read. It was a postcard from Ryder! The picture on the front was of an iguana with a note on the back that explained what an iguana was and where it lived. On the bottom it was signed, Daddy.

'It's ugly,' she said.

On a sudden impulse Jenny said, 'Helen, would you like to go home to England?'

Helen's eyes opened wide then she ran into Jenny's arms and cried, 'I want Patty.'

\*       \*       \*

It took only a few days for Jenny to persuade the head to release her from her contract at the school. Then packing up as much as they could carry, Jenny booked tickets for their return flight to the UK.

She had sold her car to pay for the tickets and was reluctant to ask Margaret for a lift to the airport. As it happened it wasn't necessary.

A neighbour who was also an air hostess was driving in that morning and offered to take them with her. It meant a longer wait at the airport but Jenny didn't mind that.

Jenny was buying some sweets to suck on take off and landing and a couple of comics for Helen when a hand tapped her on the shoulder.

'Hi, there, who are you meeting?'

Jenny jumped. Dan was standing behind her, the welcoming smile slowly changing to one of question as he saw their hand luggage.

'Going somewhere?' he asked.

Helen piped up from her mother's side.

'We're going home, Uncle Dan.'

His glance swung back to Jenny, a puzzled frown on his face.

'Home?'

'To England. I kept my promise and told Ryder the truth, but he didn't want to know.'

'Does he know you're going?'

'No.'

The big man looked uncomfortable.

'I don't understand. It's not like Ryder to behave this way.'

Jenny shrugged.

'Won't you wait until he comes back from this trip? Give him a chance to explain. There must be some reason for all this.'

'No, Dan, I'm sorry. Say goodbye, Helen,' she urged the little girl, then, taking her by the hand, walked away.

111

Patty gave them a warm if surprised welcome. She fed them and fussed over them insisting that they stayed awake to tell her all about America when jet lag would have had them curl up and go to sleep. They slept finally in Patty's spare room.

The next morning Patty broke the news that her house was full.

'But I've a friend in Friar Street who can let you have a place. Not as big as the one you had here, mind, but it would do for now.'

Jenny thought of the tiny flat upstairs and had great trouble trying to visualise anything smaller. Patty was watching anxiously for Jenny's reaction.

'If you don't like the idea, you're always welcome to have the spare room until you find something else. Maybe I could ask the Jenkins to move out,' Patty said to herself.

'Of course, you can't,' a horrified Jenny objected. 'We'll go to Friar Street.'

Helen was sitting on Patty's knee and she looked up to ask, 'Will we have a swimming pool like we had at Daddy's house?'

'Well, there's posh for you.' Patty laughed. 'No, my love, we don't have houses with swimming pools around here.'

Feelings of guilt swamped Jenny, but, she reasoned, she would find work and in time a little house. All she had to do was carry on where they'd left off when they'd gone to America.

But soon that proved impossible. It had depended upon staying here with Patty who was always available for baby-sitting downstairs. The money she had set aside to keep them going until she found work soon vanished.

The flat in Friar Street was like the one in Patty's house but with only one bedroom instead of two. Tim was waiting for them one day when they returned to Patty's.

'Oh, Tim,' Jenny cried, rushing over to him and flinging her arms around his neck.

Tim wiggled his eyebrows at Helen where she danced up and down behind her mother, waiting for her turn to push between them.

There were tears in Jenny's eyes when she stepped back from him. Then she noticed how different he looked. He had filled out over the summer, lost the rangy look. His skin was smooth and still slightly tanned. He wasn't her immature Tim anymore.

'How did you know we were here?'

'I phoned him,' Patty admitted.

Tim placed Helen back on the floor.

'I thought we could go out for the day, catch up on all the news.'

Jenny gave him a sad smile and nodded.

There was a car outside by the kerb, second-hand but shiny. He took them to the park by the river and while they talked, Helen ran ahead scuffing the falling leaves of autumn.

'Patty tells me she has no room for you,' Tim said.

'We found a place just around the corner.'

'Have you got a job?'

'Give me a chance, Tim. We've only just arrived.'

'I know, only I thought perhaps that was what had brought you home, the offer of a job.'

'No. I need to find one quickly.'

'There's a position in the school I work in. Twelve to thirteen year olds. Big classes though, inner city, bit on the rough side. But if you think you can handle it I'll put a word in for you.'

'I'd be grateful, Tim, for anything to tide me over.'

It was several weeks later when Jenny had the offer of a larger flat. She had drawn her first salary from the school she now worked at with Tim. It was hard, thankless work but the money was welcome. They used Tim's car to ferry hers and Helen's few possessions to the other side of town. The new flat was unfurnished and it was while they were laughing over the task of fitting a carpet Jenny had bought in a sale and that now turned out to be far too big that there was a loud knocking on the outside door.

Jenny got up and ran down the stairway to

answer it. She was attempting, with dirty hands, to rub a smut from her face as she threw open the door. Her knees weakened to the point of collapse when she saw Ryder standing there.

He looked her up and down, a scowl on his face, and a crumpled parcel of flowers in one hand. After the initial shock she felt hysterical laughter run up her throat but before it had time to escape, he was talking to her.

'Well, aren't you going to invite me in? I've had to drag over half the city looking for you. I found Patty eventually and she told me you were in the process of moving.'

He was stepping over the threshold as he spoke.

'Who is it, Jen? Do you need any help?' Tim called down from the head of the stairs.

Ryder threw his head back to look up at the younger man.

'No, she doesn't and it's her husband.'

He thrust the flowers into her hands and turned to go. In the time it took Jenny to recover her wits, Ryder had climbed into a grey saloon and started the engine. She called after him through a blur of tears but the car pulled out into the traffic and was gone.

When she came out of school the following day, she could have sworn she saw the same car parked across the road but she had to run to catch her bus. Patty had insisted on keeping Helen overnight. There was a children's film on at the local cinema after tea that the little girl wanted to see.

A note was pushed under her door when Jenny arrived home. It was from Ryder asking her to have dinner with him that evening at eight o'clock. Some devil prompted her to dress in the same outfit that had so enraged Ryder on her evening out with Kane. She was having second thoughts about it when he knocked at the door. It was too late to change.

His eyes narrowed as he took in the picture before him. Then without a word he was holding out his hand. She pulled on her coat and turned to shut the door. She felt his hand slip under her elbow but she refused to look up. He ushered her into the car and climbed into the driving seat and they were off into the heart of the city. It had been dark for some time when they stopped at last in front of a tall, Edwardian house.

The recognition was instant. The horror and distaste for the cold, heartless house was still with her despite the passing of years. How could he bring her back here, to the place where all the misery had begun? She squeezed shut her eyes, then, taking a deep breath, masked her expression and climbed out of the car.

'I was under the impression I was being asked out to dinner. Don't tell me Mrs Mould is still in residence.'

'I think you'll find there have been a few

changes since you were last here.'

As they approached the entrance, the lights came on in the front of the house and the door was opened wide. A young girl with a long blonde plait and dressed in a smart grey dress welcomed them inside.

Jenny muffled the gasp of astonishment in her throat as she gazed around the light airy hall. White paint covered the once dark woodgrain and the stained glass panels in the doors glowed warmth across the cream walls. The wood floors were uncovered, the mellow oak lightened and polished to a fine finish.

They handed over their coats and made their way into the lounge. Here again the change was dramatic. Jenny sat down on one of the two settees that embraced the open fire as Ryder crossed the room to a drinks cabinet.

'Sherry?' he queried.

'Why not. Are we to eat here?'

'You have some objections?'

'No, not at all. I wasn't aware that you still owned the house.'

She blushed as he handed over her glass. It wasn't any of her business what he did with his property or his money, not any more. The meal was good, the conversation stilted but polite and still neither had broached the subject of their last parting.

The girl waiting on them was hired in from a firm of caterers who specialised in small, private contracts. They would open up a house and prepare a meal for a visiting owner who didn't want to keep a full-time staff. After the meal, they went back to the lounge, sitting one on either side of the fire, cups of coffee in their hands.

'When did you have all this done?' Jenny asked, indicating her surroundings with a wave of her hand.

'I decided to keep the house on after Dad died. I had the work started before we left for America. It will be more comfortable and more convenient for the airport than some inner city hotel. I don't intend to lose track of you again even if you do decide to instigate a divorce.'

Jenny's head jerked up.

'I've never mentioned divorce.'

He put down his cup with a clatter of china.

'I want you back, Jenny, on any terms,' he said holding her startled stare. 'I can give you more than that boy at the top of stairs ever could. I know he asked you to marry him, Patty told me, but he's not for you.'

Jenny's mouth made a protesting gasp.

'You can't talk to me like that, you . . . you, jumped up . . . '

He was out of his seat and pulling Jenny from hers.

'I was angry, Jennifer,' he said holding her away from him. 'I was so angry when I came back all those months ago and saw you standing there in that dingy flat doorway, a

118

beautiful, mature mother of a five-year-old daughter, whom I knew was mine the minute I saw her. I couldn't trust myself to look at you let alone speak to you. Do you have any idea what you did to me? You and my father between you. Have you ever given any thought to how different our lives could have been over the past empty years had I known of Helen's existence, let alone what it would have meant to the child?'

Jenny was shaking her head.

'Of course I did. I wanted to tell you but your work always came first. If you knew she was yours why have you been pretending that she wasn't?'

'I waited to hear from you for weeks, months, after I first went to America, sure that you would contact me but when time passed and you didn't I suppose I was punishing you, making you wait, as I had.'

Dark eyes stared down into her light ones.

'The waiting is over, Jenny. I'm asking you again, will you come to America with me, as my wife? Will you give us a second chance? The waiting time is over.'

Jenny nodded.

'I never stopped loving you, you know,' she whispered.

'Nor I you,' he murmured as he swept her into his arms.

MS